IT TAKES TWO

IT TAKES
TWO

EDITED BY
RACHEL KRAMER BUSSEL

CLEiS
PRESS

Published in the United States by Cleis Press, an imprint of Start Midnight, LLC, 221 River Street, Ninth Floor, Hoboken, New Jersey 07030.

Printed in the United States
Cover design: Jennifer Do
Cover image: Shutterstock
Text design: Frank Wiedemann

First Edition.
10 9 8 7 6 5 4 3 2 1

Trade paper ISBN: 978-1-62778-328-6
E-book ISBN: 978-1-62778-541-9

Contents

INTRODUCTION:
LUST FOR LIFE

When I came up with the idea for *It Takes Two*, I was inspired in part by being in a long-term relationship, and by knowing that many erotica readers are themselves coupled up and looking to see characters like them reflected on the page. The couples you'll meet within these stories are adventurous, wild, and ready to go there, whether that means a hotel room where they ogle another couple, a kink camp, or outer space.

They're also willing to go there in a more intimate sense, with each partner allowing their other half to see them at their most naked, raw, and vulnerable. These characters let down their barriers and pursue their sexual passions alongside the person who knows them best. They trust that their partner will treasure the gift of their desires, honoring them while sometimes spurring them on to be even naughtier, saying the filthy thing that's lurking in their minds that they've never spoken aloud.

In these stories, we see that the shared history of these couples is what allows them to do things they might not otherwise agree to. In "Skin Deep" by Angela Addams, in which the narrator's naked body gets painted in the most sensual way, she writes, "I let my mind wander as you coat me with your ideas, remembering the first time you brought me to orgasm with your brilliance." That history plays a role in each of these stories, but it's what's happening right now that's sure to turn you on.

You'll find everything from fetishes to BDSM to sex toys, dirty talk, role-playing, threesomes, and more in these pansexual stories. The erotic takes a science fiction turn in "Out of Orbit" by R. Magdalen, where special suits help a couple separated in space feel each other's bodies and get each other off. I hope the nineteen tales in *It Takes Two* transport and arouse you, and show you just some of the ways those in couples can make passion take center stage.

Rachel Kramer Bussel
Atlantic City

ALL IS FAIR

Rae Shawn

The moment our trainer stepped out, I took advantage of my time. As of late, I hadn't spent many of my waking moments with my boyfriend. Roshaun finished another set of deadlifts and was taking a quick water break.

"Hey, Ro." I placed the tips of my fingers on his shoulder blade, slowly, allowing him to take in the feel of each pad before I dropped the next one against his skin. "We're almost done with the individualized portion of our workout. Bet I outdo you when it comes time for the joint effort."

He shifted, slipping his arm around my waist, and pulled me flush against him. "Moni, let me explain this to you quick and simple; if we racing, I'll let you win."

"Yeah?" I pressed even closer, staring at the smile curving his luscious brown lips. "Why?"

"Because I don't mind coming second."

My eyes jumped to his, quirking an eyebrow when I found the twinkle there. "In that case, let's get in position."

"I've still got another round to do and so do you. X ain't about to—"

"My wife went into labor!" X called as he banged the door open. "Roshaun, this is your gym anyway. Finish your workout or head home, I don't care. We'll pick it up in a day or two. I've got to go."

"No need for explanation," I called toward him. "Give her our love."

He snatched up his belongings as I said, "And congrats again."

"Thanks, Monica." He paused in the door frame. "Y'all are supposed to be doing that last set; don't be in here getting freaky. Y'all way too close."

"She's my girl. I'll fuck her against every machine, wall, and table if I please," Ro said.

"I really don't need that mental image." X threw up the deuces before the door shut behind him.

"It appears we don't have to do that workout after all," I said.

"You're right." He swiveled our bodies, pushing me against the wall that had been at his back. "Yet, I do want to work you out. I'm still positive you'll come first."

"Bet I can get you to come from the things you do to me. The way my voice'll hitch. The moans, and squeezes, our eyes connecting as you put me on top to ride you. I'm sure you'll tumble over the edge first."

He grabbed my thigh, lifting it until I hooked my knee around his hip. It put me off-kilter because I had to raise up on my tip toes to do it. I knew why he liked me like this; it gave him more control.

"Yeah? Well, neither of us are on the field, but how about we sweeten the pot?" he suggested.

His fingers danced up my bare leg. Wearing shorts seemed

appropriate when we were working out, but now? The heat radiating from between my legs had to be setting his crotch ablaze. My eyes melted closed and a soft moan escaped me. The feeling of his palm sliding to grip my ass sent my heart rate to dangerous levels. No matter what this man did, his touch, his attention, everything turned me on. Especially the feeling of his erection growing just beneath the sweats he wore.

"What did you have in mind?"

"How about you go put on that sexy lingerie you wear on the field and I'll get in my dressed down gear. If you can score a touchdown, I'll give you anything you want."

"When I win, I'll have you put that tongue right where I want it—moving from surface to surface up in here—before we go home and I fuck your brains out."

"*When?*" He fought a smile. "Okay, well . . . *when* I win, I'm bending you over the counter that lines the windows overlooking the park and cityscape. I'll stare at the reflected lust in your eyes as we watch the moon cross the sky."

"Shit, I might have to let you win if that's the treat I get."

He leaned down and kissed me, our mouths molding together like they were made for one another. The sweet mint of his toothpaste blasting my senses. The warm stroke of his tongue against mine. The gnashing of teeth when we both moved in the same direction. I chuckled and pulled back. "Okay, okay. Let's get dressed so we can do this."

"Inside or on the actual field?" he asked, releasing my leg and righting my body.

I watched his eyes dart across my face, searching for my answer. He might be one of the most important players on his team—their shutdown cornerback—but when it came to me, he let me lead where we'd go. That included who'd be in charge in the bedroom. "Let's go out there. Really up the stakes."

Since mostly athletes used the gym, we housed practice gear and extra uniforms. Attached to the gym was a full-sized track and football field. It was private and only used by our teams or groups that reserved it. Our competitive asses were about to head outside in the dead of winter to see where this led. To see who would win and which fantasies were about to become realities.

Once I had on my cheeky underwear and bra, I pulled on the thickest socks I could find in my locker and a pair of cleats. I walked out to find him shirtless, that slim figure waiting for me to run my hands across it. His athletic tights were low on his hips and he'd put on thick socks and cleats as well.

"Ready to get your ass handed to you?" I walked toward the door that led to the field.

He rushed up behind me, pinning my front to the cold metal. I sucked in a shuddering breath, but with his heat and hard-as-stone dick against my back, my body was confused.

"Sorry, but you said something about asses and hands, and I couldn't pass up the opportunity to have yours in mine." He squeezed generous amounts of both cheeks while placing a kiss on my temple. I giggled. Pushing back against him, he let me free and pulled the door open for us.

"First to score wins," he said once we were on the field. I grabbed a football from the bag on the sideline.

"What kinda score are we going after again?" I let all of the seduction seep into my tone.

"Touchdown, baby girl." He got into position. "I'll let you have your four downs before you turn over the ball and I get my shot."

"I'm glad you think I need all four downs." I dropped into my stance. At the twenty-five-yard line on what would be considered his side, I looked at how far I had to go. This would be thrilling. The cold air whipped around us. My pussy clenched as my nipples tightened. I was sure the temperature wasn't the only thing that had my body reacting.

His gaze roamed over me and I was honestly ready to accidentally fumble the ball so I could have him fucking me ASAP. My competitive brain snuck through my sex-fog and said no. Clearing my mind, I called out a play like we were really in the middle of a game. A smile graced his beautiful face.

"Come on, Moni. Quit stalling." His hands rested on top of his thighs.

I said "hike" and went to spin past him. He caught me around my waist and pulled me to the ground, his body on top of mine. I stuck my tongue out and he sucked it. "Nice try, babe. Wanna go again or give up?"

I pushed his shoulder and hopped to my feet, dusting brittle grass off my ass. "Second and nine. I can do this."

"Okay, show me what you got." He beckoned me forward.

Tilting my head, I lifted an eyebrow. *Oh, he's all game right now.* I tucked the ball between my thighs and saw his eyes drift to the action. Pulling a ponytail holder from my wrist, I worked my loose waves into a messy bun. I did the sexy vibe well; I knew that without a doubt. But right now was about winning. He wanted me to play, I'd play. His gaze slowly lifted to meet mine and I smirked when it did.

"You done ogling?"

"Never, but I can hold off until I strip you down."

I laughed loudly. After regaining my composure, I started another play. This time, I distracted him before juking to the left and taking off downfield. I might've been five inches shorter than him, but before I started playing for the lingerie league, I was a sprinter. I had one of the top speeds in the nation. He was a long-distance runner in high school, so he knew how to run as well, but I thought I could take him.

I was less than ten yards from the endzone when his arms wrapped around my waist and he took us to the ground. Before I hit the ground, the ball popped out and he pulled it into his side. I tried to wrestle him for it, but he used his free hand to hold me in place as his tongue roamed my neck.

"This is not fair." I moaned and squirmed. "I'm sure you don't use these tactics to beat your other opponents."

He nipped my neck before pulling back. "All is fair in sex and football, Moni. Get with the program."

Oh, that's how it was, eh? "All right. Got it."

He rose to his feet and got in his stance. I dusted myself off again, tightening my ponytail as the adrenaline really started coursing through my body. Time to play dirty—well, more like flirty.

I stuck my ass out and leaned slightly at an angle so he could catch a tiny glimpse. The way his eyes darted, I knew he had. He called out the play and went to rush past me. I pressed my chest out, grabbed him underneath his arm, and pulled him to me. Up on my tiptoes, I brought his mouth to mine. For a split second he fought the kiss, but broke down and wrapped me in his arms.

The embrace deepened and when I felt both of his hands roaming my back, I knew he dropped the ball. I took my lips from his and worked my feathery soft kisses down his neck and chest. He watched me as I descended, my eyes glued to his until I reached the band of his tights. He tasted of salt and pinewood. The smell alone was intoxicating.

Out of the corner of my eye, I caught sight of the ball. Before he could notice what I was doing, I scrambled toward it, picked it up, and ran into the endzone. I cheered, bouncing up and down in circles.

"That was outright fucked up, Moni."

The laugh that bubbled over couldn't be stopped. I stared at him, catching my breath. "You said all is fair in sex and football. I scored a touchdown, big boy. So, it's time to give me what I want."

"Okay, fine. A win is a win and to be honest, tonguing you down has been on my mind all day."

He closed the yards between us, but I put up a hand. "No. I'm sweaty and so are you. Hit the showers, big boy. Then we can have some real fun."

He groaned but listened. He tossed the football back toward the bag where I'd grabbed it and we went inside to shower; me in the ladies' locker room and him in the men's—just in case someone came in for a late-night workout, which likely wouldn't happen and didn't much matter since we were about to fuck in every inch of this building.

While toweling down my hair, I heard his groan of appreciation. I was stark naked, still dripping and facing the mirror. He could see all of me without a problem. Through the reflection, I saw he hadn't gotten dressed either. A towel rested dangerously low on his hips.

He stepped up behind me, his hand relaxing on the small of my back before he slid it higher and gently bent me into a tabletop position.

"Let me start your reward by sopping up this water right here." His hand smoothed over my hip and tugged me back, spreading my legs with a kick of his foot as he set me up just how he wanted.

"Ready to get your wish, baby girl?" His head dipped down. His fingers ran against my pussy lips and I almost jumped out of my skin. This was what I wanted—him touching me in places that were usually pleased in the confines of our home.

"God, yes."

I heard him shift before his tongue ran up my inner thigh. I breathed out an "Oh," gripping the counter for leverage. He'd barely started, but I knew it wasn't anywhere close to what he had in store for me.

When his tongue circled my outer lips from behind, I had to keep myself calm, I couldn't come yet. I refused to let it be over that quickly. Plus, I'd said the way he wound me up would have him coming without me even touching him. I could make that happen as well. I just had to focus.

The moment his tongue slipped between my lips and curved against my clit, I knew I was about to lose this part of our bet. No matter how hard I wanted to front, he knew what he was doing. He was damn good at it too. He just . . . knew. I could feel the smile trying to grace his beautiful face because he was clearly aware of exactly how he was winding up my body.

My eyes fluttered shut. He knew me better than I knew myself and I couldn't begin to be upset that he treated my body like the palace that it was. After teasing and probing just enough to get me wetter than a waterfall, he turned around and slung my thighs over his shoulders. He held me to his face as he really went to work, licking like he'd never get another meal, feasting like he'd never taste anything as good ever again.

The way his beard burned my inner thighs felt like heaven. The warmth of his tongue, the angles he used to slip it inside me. The outright girth. The way he rolled the massive, long thing as he did his best work and moaned his appreciation, I wasn't sure how many more seconds I would last.

My legs started shaking. My foot pressed against his back. He leaned away slightly, a chuckle escaping him. "Thought I was going to come first from the way you made me feel."

"Well, tell your tongue . . . " I took a breath and worked to get my brain to find the words that had run away. While I was attempting a retort, he reattached that naughty mouth of his to me. Whatever I was in the process of saying died and I wasn't even upset.

Before I could come he lifted me to a standing position. "I don't think you want to release your inhibitions in the bathroom. Let me mash our fantasies together and finish eating you out properly." He rose to his feet and pulled me up to wrap my wobbly legs around his waist. He grabbed the towel I'd completely forgotten about and covered my back with it.

"To the windows we go."

"Did you ever think we'd get down in the gym before tonight?" I asked, voice audibly shaky. My arms wrapped around his neck as he guided us through the low-lit room.

"I thought about it the moment I bought this place. I wanted to take you on every single surface. The best type of christening, but this right here . . . " He sat me on the counter that lined the windows. I glanced over my shoulder to see the night sky as beautiful as ever. I donned a smile which was quickly replaced by crinkled eyebrows and a straight face as his tongue tapped against my clit. "This was number one of the list of places I wanted you."

"Then make that dream a reality," I managed the moment before he went back to eating like we were about to die.

My left leg hung freely while my right foot slid down his spine. I tried to find something to hold on to, but I couldn't. He worked me up to the edge of my orgasm, my hands flying to the window behind me. I couldn't get a full moan to leave my throat, but that didn't stop him from completely destroying my senses. My body tensed. I was so close, but I couldn't come. Not yet. I had to attempt to win the first half of our bet.

"You really gonna keep that sweetness to yourself, baby girl?"

I nodded because my voice was completely gone. My chest heaved and breathing was something I had to remind myself to actively do.

"Okay, that's fine. I know you're on the edge." He wiped the corners of his mouth before grabbing his beard. "I'd love you to give me a proper glow, but I don't mind waiting. Can I bend you over this counter now?"

"You could've started with that, big boy." My words tumbled out, but I managed a grin.

He helped me down before allowing his towel to hit the floor.

I shouldn't be intimidated after all these years, but his dick put others to shame. The curve, the width, the veins that angled to rub against the inside of me. I'd craved it without seeing it, but now that it sprang to attention and the precome was glistening at his slit, I wanted him seated so deep inside of me that I could feel him in the back of my throat from my pussy. I turned around, spread my arms on the counter, and bent forward.

"Give me your best."

"We've got all night." He gripped one hip and rubbed himself against my entrance. I heard him groan and knew he'd been fighting against his own release, just as I thought. "I don't think I'll last that long and we'll need a break in between, but I'm going to give you every fantasy you've ever imagined right here in this room."

"As long as we're working through yours too, baby, I'll gladly lose sleep and the ability to think straight for a week."

He chuckled and started sliding into me. I looked at our hazed reflection on the window before my gaze shifted to the lights in the distance. When I felt him all the way in to the hilt, I clenched my pussy and rocked forward then back.

He placed his other hand on my hip to stop my movement.

"If you keep any of that up, I won't last more than a minute. Let me give it to you good. You can take me over after, baby girl."

"Then it's safe to say I won tonight."

"You win every night and so do I because you're my girl and I love you with all my heart."

"I love you, too, Roshaun."

He slid out and slammed back into me. The stars in the sky had nothing on the ones that were dancing happily through my vision and I couldn't wait for everything else we had in store. All is fair in love and football and we were going to try it all.

GETAWAY FROM THE EVERYDAY

Christina Berry

Austin sunsets are generally pretty, but tonight's is spec-
tacular. I sit in one of the two chairs situated in front of
our hotel room's floor-to-ceiling windows and watch that big
orange globe tease at the violet crown of the Hill Country to the
west of the city.

Nate is in the shower. "Washing the day away," he calls his
evening routine after work. Already showered, I nurse a whiskey as I wait for our night to get started.

People joke disparagingly about long-married couples who
schedule sex, but for us the joke is real. If we didn't schedule this
downtown rendezvous once a month, our sex life would consist
entirely of stolen moments between work and bedtime. Morn-
ing-breath perfumed quickies before the kids wake up. Three
years ago, we started this marital ritual, our "Getaway from
the Everyday." The kids love their weekend slumber party at my
sister's house with their cousins, and they never need to know
that this weekend isn't about them. It's about us. One night a

month in a hotel room downtown with no phones, no laptops, no family, no obligations—nothing but the two of us, together in whatever way the mood fits.

When we're here, it's like we're back in college, trying new things, boning like our joints don't ache and drinking like there's no hangover tomorrow. Of course, Sundays are always rough because there is a hangover, and our joints do ache. *Ugh!* When did we get so old? We're Generation X, damn it. Once upon a time we were the "Kids of America." The "Kids in the Hall." But we're not kids anymore. We're forty-something and everything hurts, *and* we're scheduling sex.

I take another gulp of my drink. The booze burns my throat as Nate comes out of a cloud of steam from the bathroom, naked and looking just as sexy as the day I married him. My mouth waters at the sight of his cock, hanging heavy between his legs as he towels his hair dry and then slips on a pair of boxer briefs.

"What are you doing over there?"

"Watching the sunset."

I glance back out as the sun kisses us good night, and the clouds pop with color. Pinks, oranges, and yellows feather across the sky all around our seventeenth-floor room, making it easy to imagine the bliss and freedom of the birds that soar and glide around us.

"Holy shit!" Nate startles me from my peaceful thoughts as he settles into the chair beside me at the window, beer in hand.

"What?" I ask, cranky and trying to calm my heart rate.

"She's handcuffed."

"What? Why? Who? Who's handcuffed?"

"You don't see them?" Nate tips his chin forward at the view out the window. It's a big city, and there are probably a couple dozen people in handcuffs out there . . . What is he talking about—

Oh!

I see. In a window of the high-rise hotel a block over, same floor as ours, same corner of the building, is a couple on the bed, the lights blazing against the twilight sky.

The woman wears nothing but a black leather blindfold over her eyes and black cuffs on her wrists. She sits on the mattress with her knees together, her feet beneath her, her back rigid, and her pert breasts pushed forward by her cuffed posture. The man is in jeans and lounges comfortably across from her, a tray of food set between them.

He's saying something to her as he peruses the tray and selects a strawberry. My breath hitches as he lifts it and presses it to the woman's lips. She slowly opens her mouth and takes a bite of the fruit.

I have to pick up my jaw from the floor to say, "Wow."

"Yeah." Nate grins wide, mischief in his eyes. He's as curious as I am.

We continue to watch them, though we probably shouldn't. Is this peeping? Are we creepers for looking? Surely not. We're simply sitting in our room looking out the window. Is it our fault someone's performing a peep show out there? If anything, they're the ones in the wrong. This is indecent exposure, right?

Indecent, sure, but *really fucking hot*. The last shards of sunlight break over the city, leaving us in the dark, and the man selects a grape to feed her next. I lean a little closer.

They're attractive. The man is tall and made of lean muscle, with light hair cut into a short mohawk and an assortment of colorful tattoos dotting his arms and back. The woman is a tiny pixie compared to her companion, with supple muscles in her legs, arms, and abs and bubblegum-pink hair braided down both sides of her neck.

The man lifts the grape to her mouth and pushes it between

her lips. The woman accepts the fruit like she's ravenous, starving. With each morsel he feeds her, she sucks the tips of his fingers into her mouth, hungry for more than just the food.

"Should we be watching this?" Nate asks. His voice is rough, thick with excitement. He's as turned on as I am.

"Why not? We're literally sitting in our hotel room, looking out the window. There's nothing wrong with that."

He chuckles. "I see you've given this some thought."

"I'm a thoughtful person." I wink at him and take a sip of my whiskey.

Nate opens his mouth like he's ready to debate, but the words die on his tongue when the man across the way moves the food tray to the nightstand and comes back with something new in his hand. *It's not food.* It's a silver, shiny butt plug. I know this because we have one just like it at home, with a cute little ruby rhinestone on the stem. We haven't played with it in . . . jeez, it's been years. Ass play doesn't easily fit into stolen-moment quickies.

My husband and I shift closer to the window as the man speaks to the woman, probably telling her to open wide but not to bite down because this isn't food and will shatter her teeth.

Nodding enthusiastically, the woman opens her mouth, and he lays the plug's heavy weight on her tongue. She closes her lips, sucking on it like a lollipop while the man moves around to her back. He uncuffs her wrists, then has her raise her arms so he can recuff her hands in front of her. The woman bends forward and balances on her hands and knees, arching her back to offer her ass up.

I know what's coming before he does it. I tense as I wait for it, like I'm the one about to be—

Smack.

Totally immersed in the scene, I jerk at the sight like I can feel it. Certain beyond reason I can hear the sound when he spanks her bare ass once, twice, again and again. The woman writhes and bucks in response, struggling not to open her mouth and cry out from the pleasure and pain. But she has to keep the plug in—clearly that's part of this game they're playing as he spanks her again and again, harder and harder.

After a moment, he stops to gently stroke his fingers over the warm red marks he's made. She shivers and relaxes just as he spanks her again. She jerks and writhes, and I can imagine that she's even wetter than I am. Nate takes a drink of his beer as he balls and flexes his empty hand on his knee, like he can feel those spankings on his own palm.

The man leans over her and whispers something into her ear. She curls closer to him, pressing her cheek against his as he tugs gently on the butt plug, and opens her mouth to let him have it. Her saliva drips from the end as he strokes it over her lips before straightening again behind her.

We can't see exactly what he's doing from this angle, but when the woman's expression changes, we know he's inserting the plug into her ass. She squirms and gasps before a smile spreads across her lips. I squirm too, feeling instantly, unbearably horny. I glance over at Nate, who looks back at me, a predatory hunger in his eyes as he adjusts his hardened cock in his briefs.

The man bends in half, ducking to where we can't see him behind her. She writhes even more as he does what I can only guess—kisses her ass, bites it, licks at her dripping pussy, presses a finger inside.

Then he straightens again and comes around to her front, his erection straining against the zipper of his jeans. Careful not to pull her hair, he unstraps the blindfold so she can see him.

She smiles as he takes her chin in his hands and pulls her up to kiss her. It's an achingly sweet kiss, a gentle connection shared between lovers. The woman seems to melt against him, her whole body lax, her hands hanging limp between them.

He pulls away from her mouth to look her in the eyes, watching her expression closely as he strokes her cheeks. Then he slaps her.

"Oh. Wow," I say, my eyes wide and unblinking, stunned.

"Damn," Nate agrees.

The woman's posture goes ramrod straight, and the man slaps the other cheek. He caresses her face again, sweetly soothing the sting. I can practically hear her purring like a contented kitten. He slaps her again, and she gasps and spasms. She leans toward him, her cheek rubbing against his palm, her fingers reaching for his erection.

The man holds her by her chin, keeping her away from him as he speaks to her, and she nods excitedly. He unzips his jeans with one hand and pulls his cock out. When he drops his grip from her chin, she falls forward onto her hands and knees again, and he shoves his cock into her eager mouth. He twists her braids around his fist as he guides her movements, and she takes everything he gives her. He pushes into the back of her throat and holds her there. Her posture changes as she struggles to breathe and tries not to choke, then he lets her go, and she comes up for air, a delicate strand of saliva connecting them.

Goddamn, this is hot.

"Watching you watch them is really turning me on," Nate says, his dilated pupils shining like onyx in the dim light. He reaches for me and strokes my cheek. He won't slap me, though. When you're intimate with someone for almost fifteen years, you know their limits, and that's one of mine. Spanking: yes. Slapping: no.

I glance over at Nate. "Do you think they know they're being watched?"

He grins out of one side of his mouth, always my favorite of his expressions, and answers, "It's after dark, their curtains are open, and they have every light on. It's fair to say exhibitionism is part of their kink." He raises a brow. "And voyeurism is part of *yours*."

I smirk, wanting to deny it, but why bother? He's right. I've watched plenty of porn through the years, and it certainly can turn me on, but never like this. This is so much more real, more intimate. There's no director demanding a change in position, no GoPro camera strapped to the guy's forehead. This is just them, fucking, and us, watching. It's like we're there, like we're a part of the scene. This intimate connection Nate and I are sharing with two complete strangers is the most exciting thing to happen in our sex life in quite some time. I feel like I should thank them or tip them for their performance. Especially when Nate sets his beer on the table behind us and slides onto his knees on the floor. He comes to me, brushing the sides of my robe aside so he can kiss and nip at my legs like he's desperate for a taste.

"What are you doing?" I ask him, as if I don't know.

"I'm going to make you come while you watch them."

"People will see."

"Our lights are off. We're in shadow. No one can see. Now, move your fine ass forward, and spread your legs for me."

I stare at him for a moment, the lust twinkling in his eyes like starlight, and slowly I set my own drink aside as I slide forward on the chair and spread my legs. Nate pounces, his mouth hot on my skin as he kisses his way up my thighs. I moan and widen my legs, lifting my hips just enough for my husband to tug my underwear off and toss it aside.

Across the way, the man fucks the woman's face harder and faster, choking her with his cock as he wraps the fingers of one hand around her throat while the other tugs at her pink braids. He pulls his cock out of her mouth, leaving her gasping as his fingers tighten on her throat. He drags her up for a kiss, his tongue filling her mouth now.

"Oh, God." I moan and clutch the arms of the chair when Nate strokes his tongue along my wet folds and presses a finger inside me.

"You're so fucking wet, baby." He groans as he slips a second finger in and starts to tease and suck on my clit.

Nate's distraction is exquisite. I lean back so I can watch it all: my husband's head between my legs while the couple across the way go at it. I tangle my fingers in Nate's sexy salt-and-pepper hair and move my hips to complement the rhythm he sets. He hums his pleasure as he strokes his tongue faster and curls his fingers inside me, touching me just right.

The man shifts the woman so she's on her hands and knees again. He strips out of his jeans as he stalks around behind her. It feels like the woman is looking right at me, but I'm sure all she can see is her own reflection in the mirror of their window. She watches the man like I do as he strokes his cock with one hand while he rubs her ass with the other.

He's rock hard, and I hold my breath as I wait for some reaction from the woman to indicate when he's penetrated her, a double penetration considering that plug in her ass. He pushes inside her with one deep thrust of his cock. I know because the woman's mouth gapes open on a silent moan.

I come instantly—hard, fast, and wet; I drench my husband's fingers. Nate's groan of delight mingles with my gasps of arousal. He continues to tease me with his fingers and mouth, wringing every drop of pleasure from me.

We stay like that for a moment, catching our breath. Nate turns his head, kissing and laving his tongue on my thigh as he watches the other couple with me. I feather my fingers through his hair, needing to touch him. We both sigh with deep satisfaction as an ecstatic expression settles on the woman's face each time the man sinks a little deeper inside her.

The man's rhythm grows faster, his strokes harder. His large fists clutch at the woman's hips as he pounds into her. He's coiled tight with tension and looks so beautiful the way the shadow of night and the lights of the room play at the edges and lines of his muscles.

I stand, and Nate drops back to watch me disrobe. I collect our drinks from the table behind us and move them to the credenza. When I return to the table, I lean forward a bit, pushing my breasts out and my ass up, an offering. Nate's hungry gaze moves over me, and he gives me that sexy half grin again.

"I need you to fuck me, Nate. Now."

Nate springs to his feet like a man half his age and peels his boxer briefs off in a flash. His erection bounces when it comes free, desperate for attention.

When he's behind me, he nudges at my ankles so I spread my legs wider, and in one solid thrust he presses his cock deep inside. I yelp at the pinch of pain and utter a streak of nonverbal noises at the intense fullness. His erection throbs inside me as he holds himself still, just for a moment, then he pulls nearly all the way out before thrusting home again.

We both stare at the window as we fuck. There is the barest hint of our own reflection in the glass. And just beyond that ghostly image, the man pounds so hard and deep into the woman she's screaming and writhing. He grabs her braids and pulls, forcing her back to arch like a bow, then speaks into her ear as he fucks her ceaselessly.

"What do you think he's saying to her?" I whisper.

Nate tangles his fingers in my hair and pulls me up, bowing

my back just like the woman's across the way. His hot breath warms my ear with each sexy gust. I can only imagine that the man's voice rumbles as deep as my husband's when he says, "There's a whole city out there watching me fuck you. They all want you, but you're mine, aren't you?"

"Yes." I answer like I'm her.

"You're my little fuck toy to play with."

"Yes."

"I'm going to use every inch of you tonight."

Unlike the other couple, we didn't bring a butt plug to our party, but we did pack lube, and Nate wets one of his fingers and works his hand between us so he can press the finger at the entrance of my ass, making it clear which inch he means. I gasp and whimper at the new sensation and try to relax my muscles.

Nate's voice is slightly softer when he asks, "Will you give me everything I want?"

"Yes." I moan as he strokes his finger another knuckle deeper and fucks me harder and faster.

"You'll take it all and love every fucking minute of it, won't you, Cassandra?" *My name.* He's not speaking for the other man anymore. This is my husband speaking to me.

"Yes," I answer in a rough voice, sounding as desperate as I feel. "I love it. I love you."

Behind me, my husband starts to build a rhythm. His finger still teases my ass as his cock takes my pussy in long, hard strokes. God, I love the way he fucks me. It's sweet yet demanding. He wants all of me, and I gladly give it. The couple across the way is quickly forgotten, my attention completely absorbed by everything Nate is doing to me.

"Play with your clit. I want you to come again before I fuck your ass."

I whimper at the raw sound of his voice and the brashness of

his words, but I do what I'm told, using my fingers to stimulate
my clit while he works the rest of me.

Nate presses extra deep inside me then stills. Hugging me
in his arms, holding me impaled on his cock, he pushes a second finger into my ass, getting me ready for him. Then, oh, so
slowly, he starts to move inside me again. It's too good, divine
torture, overwhelming in all the right ways.

We stand in the dark, tangled together, connected so exqui-
sitely. I soon shatter like glass. He holds me up as the orgasm
courses through me in hot waves. While I'm still coming, he
teases my ass with cold droplets of lube and the slide of his
fingers before easing out of my pussy and pressing into my ass.

I scream, ready for him, but never quite prepared for that first
thrust. It's like I'm bursting out of my skin, too much sensation
all at once, an explosive combustion burning me from the inside
out. I struggle to remain standing, clawing my nails into Nate's
hair just to hold on. He slowly pushes deeper, moving in coaxing
strokes, urging me to take him in. My orgasm peaks again, still
rolling through me as he fucks my ass harder and faster.

Nate grunts sexy sounds into my ear while he revels in the
tightness of my ass. And God, the way he fills me, it's almost too
much . . . almost. But with each stroke, my body relaxes until
the sensation is pure ecstasy, a perfect driving rhythm that sends
pleasure sparking through every nerve in my body. After a few
moments of relentless pounding, he stills. His fingers claw into
my hips as he comes hard, bellowing and collapsing against me,
his head on my shoulder, his weight heavy on my back. In gusts
of hot air across my cheek he tells me, "I love you so fucking
much, Cassandra Marie Hart."

Is there anything sweeter or sexier then hearing those words
from the man you've spent most of your adult life with, the
father of your children, the man who just reamed your ass?

"I love you too, ass fucker."

He laughs and slowly pulls out of me. I turn in his arms to hug him, and we balance together like that for a moment, our knees hardly holding us up, so we hold each other up. As we move toward the shower, I shut the curtains, not interested anymore in the couple across the way. The rest of our "Getaway from the Everyday" isn't out there; it's right here.

LITTLE RED
GOES TO
KINK CAMP

Jodie Griffin

"I have a surprise for you, Little Red."

At the familiar voice behind me, I set the box I'd brought in from the car onto the kitchen table and turned slowly, my stomach clenching with the heady combination of nerves and anticipation. I dropped my gaze to the floor at his feet. "Thank you, Master."

He cupped my chin and lifted it, meeting my eyes and grinning that arrogant grin of his, the one that made me quake in my boots but also made me wet. "You don't even know what it is yet. You may regret thanking me before the night is out."

Entirely possible, because Zev was thoroughly sadistic. Then again, I was every inch his masochistic counterpart, so maybe not. Either way, whatever kinky gameplay he came up with? I was all in, which would surprise no one. "Yes, Master."

He laughed. "You have ten minutes to shower. Don't be late, or you'll be wearing my handprints on your ass later tonight as we greet guests." He nipped my nose, then dropped his words to a sexy growl. "And nothing else."

Was it *bad* that I considered taking eleven minutes?

Probably.

In the bathroom, I kicked off my boots and peeled down my filthy jeans, tossing them to the corner. It had been a hot and sweaty day schlepping supplies around the remote farm where Zev and a few other masters ran Kink Camp every summer. Totally worth it, though. I'd first met him here, three years ago this month, and it had become my favorite play space.

I washed thoroughly but quickly, then stepped out of the shower and reached for a towel, but the rack was empty.

"Problem, little one?"

I whirled around so quickly that my thick hair rained droplets everywhere. "I, uh . . . no towels?"

"Mmm, no." Zev pushed away from the wall, then pulled me to him, spinning me so my wet back pressed against his front and I could see us both in the mirror behind the sink. He'd also showered—his gray and black hair was still wet, and he now wore a tight black T-shirt and cargo pants. A vacation beard shadowed his face, striking against his deep olive skin, making his I'm-going-to-eat-you-up smile seem even more dangerous. He slid his big hand through my long red hair, squeezing it in his fist, and water streamed down his arm.

"What are you doing?" I protested, trying to move away. "You're going to get all wet."

"Settle down," he growled, then tucked his muscled forearm between my breasts and wrapped his palm around my throat, gripping it lightly. I shivered, goosebumps rising on my pale skin. His gaze locked on mine and, as though I'd only been waiting for his assertion of dominance over me, I stopped struggling, leaning back into him, trusting him to hold me. He made a low noise of approval, a sound I loved and craved, then rubbed his thumb over the pulse in my neck. "There we go. That's better, love."

He nipped my ear, then dug into his pocket. When I saw what he held up, a low hiss escaped. He raised a brow and I flushed, but I stayed still as he added small picnic basket–shaped bells to my nipple rings. I bit my lip to stop myself from making another sound, but when he touched them and set them moving, I couldn't help but groan at the sensation. He flashed a wicked grin, then stepped back and motioned to the door that led out of the cabin. "Your surprise is in the clearing. Let's go."

I blinked. Not because we were heading outside—playing in the open air was half the fun of Kink Camp. But . . .

I looked down at myself. "I'm all wet."

"I bet you are," he teased, deliberately misunderstanding me. He slapped my ass, his hand making a loud smacking sound on my wet skin, along with a sting that made me jump—which made the bells jangle. "Move it, Red."

I moved, my nipples throbbing with every step, setting off a matching throb deep inside my core. But when I entered the grassy circle that sat in the center of all the cabins, my muscles locked, stopping me in my tracks. Had I thought I was all in with whatever he chose? Because holy shit.

Zev came around in front of me, tipping my face up to him, blocking the source of my instant stress from my view. His beautiful amber eyes grew solemn, and his big body stilled. "Do you trust me?"

More than I ever thought I'd trust another human being. There were no signs of frustration or annoyance on his face, not that there ever were when it came to things like this, which was one of the reasons I trusted him so much. "Yes, Master. But—"

He relaxed a fraction, and his gorgeous eyes crinkled at the corners. "I know this is a soft limit for you, love. I'm asking you to trust that I'll make this good for you, but the choice is yours. You have your safewords, and you *know* I expect you to use them if you need to. You can call red right now, and I'll be fine with your decision." As though to emphasize it, he ran his knuckles softly down my cheek and smiled so gently that my heart clenched. "I promise."

He stepped out of the way and let me look again, not rushing me to decide. It was his job as my master to push my soft limits, to give me the things he thought I needed or wanted but was too afraid to ask for, but he didn't ever try to influence my decision, and he'd never betrayed my trust by ignoring a hard limit.

I took a deep breath, then blew it out slowly. "I'll try, Master."

He nodded once, but didn't say anything else, just took my hand and led me to the medium-sized rectangular metal cage sitting in the center of the clearing. It hadn't been there earlier, because I'd definitely have noticed it. The top was low enough I'd have to either kneel or sit in it. Padding covered the whole bottom and a thick wedge cushion sat at one end. On the top of the cage lay several hanks of red rope.

He moved around the cage to the back, then crouched in the grass. "Into the cage, and keep those pretty eyes on me while you do it."

I took a deep breath, then got on my hands and knees and crawled toward him, my pulse pounding in my ears, my gaze locked with his, freaked out enough about a damn *cage* that I barely noticed the nipple weights pulling.

Zev continued speaking, his voice dropping an octave, his eyes bright with satisfaction and a little bit of pride. "You're doing great, love. Come here," he said, patting the cushion and pointing. "I want you on your back, leaning on this wedge."

As he directed, I spread my legs in a wide V, my knees bent

and my feet almost touching the corners. He moved around the cage, putting his hands through the widely-spaced bars to tie the rope around my ankle. The binding on it was snug—wonderfully so, and just the way I liked it—but the way he tied it off to the cage was not. He winked, and the dimple in his cheek flashed. "Tight, but loose." Then he did the same to the other.

My heart fluttered, and the breath caught in my chest eased a bit. God, I loved this man who understood me so well. Still, my voice shook. "Th-thank you, Master."

I was able to move my legs a few inches away from the side, but that was it. I had no idea what else he had planned for me, trapped in a cage in a grassy, sunlit clearing in the woods, but I wished it included a towel, because I was already leaving a puddle under me, and not just because I hadn't been allowed to dry off after the shower.

"I'm not going to restrain your hands, Little Red." A tiny frisson of disappointment went through me, but then his wicked dimple flashed again. "*You're* going to do that by holding onto the bars behind your head."

Oh, damn. Verbal restraints were hot as fuck but so hard for me to comply with and he knew it, the sadist. He proved it with his next words.

"If you let go of the bars, there will be a *very* public punishment later. Am I clear?"

A shiver ran through me at the steel in his voice even as a dark need, one only he knew how to stoke, shuddered through me. "Y-yes, Master." I lifted my hands over my head and grasped the bars. They were warm to the touch from the sun, and I held onto them, hoping I could follow his rules—and also hoping I failed. I hated public punishments, but the paradox of my particular masochistic streak meant that the erotic humiliation of them also turned me into a seething mass of need.

His snort told me he knew exactly what I was thinking.

He walked all the way around the cage, his eyes running carefully over every inch of my body, assessing me. "Any discomfort?"

More proof of his love for me, not that I needed it; he showed me every day in a million different ways. I licked my lips. "No, Master."

"Excellent." Those eyes turned predatory. "Now, Little Red, what kind of predicament have you gotten yourself into? You should know better than to wander through the Big Bad Wolf's forest all by yourself. He's a wily one, that Wolf, setting traps for unsuspecting little girls." He ran a finger up the sole of my naked foot and I jerked, making the cage—and the bells attached to my nipples—rattle. "Shh. If you make too much noise, he'll find you before you can be rescued."

My heart stuttered. *Wolf?* Oh, damn. Master Wolf was Zev's best friend, and he'd earned that Big Bad Wolf reputation of his.

Before I could say another word, Zev stood and moved around the cage so he was beside me. I looked up, and saw him looking down at me between my hands. Grinning, he knelt down on one knee, fisted his fingers in my hair so I couldn't turn my head away from him, then lightly scratched my side with his nails, his fingers heading north. "Don't let go," he reminded me, and then he tickled me along the side of my breast.

My whole body twitched, the bells jingled, and the cage rattled again. I whimpered, the sound turning Zev's amber eyes to fire.

"Well, well, well. What have we here?"

The man who'd just spoken had a gravelly voice that always made me shiver, even when it wasn't directed at me. Master Wolf, the only dominant I knew who was more sadistically creative than my own master.

"I was hoping I'd find a sweet morsel in my trap. And here

you are. You know how the story goes, don't you, Red? The Big
Bad Wolf always eats the little girl who strays into his territory."

Zev let my hair loose, and I turned my face to the voice, my
throat going dry. Master Wolf's rich brown skin gleamed in the
late afternoon sunlight, and his dark eyes held mine, making it
impossible to look away. He was dressed all in black, a stern set
to his mouth. He had a black leather strip wrapped around his
hand, but I couldn't see what it was and I knew better than to ask.

Zev wasn't one to share me with other men and, while he
often asked Wolf—and only Wolf—to provide extra hands during our scenes, I didn't think that was what was going on here.
My heart raced anyway. Zev reached into the cage again and
squeezed my breast, and I yelped. He *tsked*. "I told you if you
made too much noise, I wouldn't be able to rescue you. Looks
like I was right."

Master Wolf spoke again. "You're lucky I've already eaten,
Little Red, so you're safe from *my* teeth this time. But you're all
nicely tied up, and my pup here needs to learn how to be a wolf.
Come close, pup, so she can see you."

Pup? He stepped aside and my eyes flew wide.

Daisy, my partner in submissive shenanigans, was naked and
on her hands and knees in the thick grass just behind him. She
wore a collar attached to the leather leash he held. A headband
with soft-looking pointed ears sat in her curly black hair and,
as she turned in a circle, I could see she was wearing a fluffy
butt plug. She shook her ass, and the tail swayed. The smell of
sunscreen wafted over to me, explaining the extra-glossy sheen
to her light-brown skin.

She crawled forward and stopped at the door to the cage,
looked up at Master Wolf and grinned, then opened her mouth
and howled.

My laugh almost burst free, but it died as Master Wolf guided her into the cage, his hand on her ass. "That's my pup. After all your hard work today, you deserve a treat. And what better treat than a juicy little girl who wanders into our woods without permission. You know the rule, pup. We eat whatever we trap." He slapped her ass over the tail, making her yelp. "Have at her."

When her tongue touched my ankle, I let out a moan. When her teeth nipped the soft skin on the inside of my knee, I gasped. And when she nibbled and licked up the inside of my thigh, lapping up the water droplets from my shower, I started to shake.

Zev knelt outside the cage, reaching in with a crop and slapping my breasts just as Daisy tongued my clit. My back arched, and I was glad I had the bars to hold onto.

I looked over at him, but aside from a hint of a twinkle that said he was enjoying himself, his face remained impassive, his voice chiding. "Eyes on Master Wolf."

Demon Dom. I wanted to look at Daisy. It had been a long time since I'd been with another woman, since I'd seen one between my thighs, her lips slick with my desire. But I did as ordered, just in time to see Master Wolf use the strap he'd been holding on Daisy's ass. She yelped, and her tongue slid deeper inside me. This time, I groaned.

Then he did it again. Each time he struck her, she fucked me with her tongue. Each time she fucked me with her tongue, my body coiled tighter and tighter. But as I neared the point of no return, everything just . . . stopped. I cried out, my frustrated body throbbing with unsatisfied need. "Master, *please.*"

"Not yet," Zev said softly, reaching between the bars to slip an eye mask over my head. "Can you see anything?"

My breath rasped in and out as the world went dark around me—another thing I both loved and loathed. I took a deep breath to settle my nerves. With my sight gone, I heard Master Wolf talking softly to Daisy, though I couldn't make out his words. I felt the faint stirring of a summer breeze against my damp flesh. I smelled green grass and earth and trees. I tasted the salt of my own tears. But I saw only darkness. "No, Master."

Even though I expected something to happen, I jolted when hands touched me. It wasn't just two hands on my body, either. One hand stroked down my thigh while another played in my belly button. A third hand drew a finger up the sole of my foot, making me jerk my leg in response, and another fucked fingers into me while yet another pinched my nipple. They roamed all over my body, petting me and pinching me and stroking me, stopping every time I got close to going over.

After the fourth time being edged, it got harder and harder to hold onto the bars. I couldn't handle it anymore, and I was in a space where I didn't want to defy Zev. "Yellow, Master."

Everything stopped, though hands remained on my body, anchoring me.

"Good girl for using your safeword. Stop, or pause?"

I licked my lips and swallowed hard. "Please, can you tie my hands?"

Maybe because I was blindfolded, I heard his indrawn breath. "Are you sure, love?"

I understood his hesitation. Completely tied up *and* blindfolded *and* locked in a cage? I had to be out of my mind. I was, but it wasn't with fear, it was with need. I felt a deep desire to give up total control to this man, to trust that by caging me and restraining me, he meant to set me free. "Yes, Master. *Please.*"

He made quick work of it. Like my legs, he bound my wrists tightly, but loose against the cage, one in each corner. I could move them slightly, but I couldn't break free. I tugged and tugged and my heart sped up, but his hand against my cheek calmed me, and his growled words made my heartbeat settle. "My brave girl."

The stroking started again. Wearing the mask and not having to remember to hold on made it easier to sink deeper into the lush sensations of hands on my body, but things took a turn when something fat and slick was pushed against and then into my ass. I tried to twist away, but tied as I was, I couldn't. A single breath later, a soft, wet tongue danced over my clit and through the arousal that coated my thighs. *Daisy.* She kept up the stroking, and then I felt her tongue slide inside me. Suddenly she stopped, crying out.

"Oh, no." She dropped her head against my stomach, and I could feel her whole body trembling. "*Master Wolf.*"

"Oh, yes. Ass up, pup. Show Master Zev what a good girl you are at holding off an orgasm even with a vibrating plug in your ass. And finish your meal. If you stop, you won't get to come at all tonight."

Just as her tongue touched me again, the plug in *my* ass started to vibrate, too. I jerked in my bonds, and fingers flicked my nipples. Zev's voice rumbled in my ear. "Do not move."

Impossible. There was no way I was going to be able to stay still, and even less of a chance I wouldn't have a screaming orgasm, but then everything stopped again. Tears seeped from my eyes and words flew from my mouth, begging, pleading ones. "Oh, God. Please, I need to come. Please. *Please.*"

I hated it when I was reduced to this—and I also loved it. Why I was wired this way, I had no idea, but Zev understood what made me burn, and he'd made a science out of breaking me down and putting me back together again so I could get the release I needed.

"Since you begged so prettily," he murmured, kissing one bound hand, "you can come. But not until *after* Daisy comes."

Master Wolf snorted. "You make Red come first, pup, and then you can have yours."

Both she and I groaned at the same time. Our demon doms didn't play fair at all, did they? One of us was going to lose, and it was probably going to be me, since I couldn't do anything but lay there and take it. My head thrashed back and forth as Daisy doubled her efforts. Everything in me wound tight and I knew I was about to lose control, but Master Wolf must've done something because Daisy lurched forward and let out a sob, and I felt her hands on my thighs start to tremble. Her teeth bit into the flesh around my clit, and the pain pushed me over the edge right with her.

For several long minutes, we lay together, her head against my thigh, her hands grasping my hips, breathing as though we'd both just run a long race. Zev took off my blindfold and I blinked at him, and then at Master Wolf when Daisy let out a long shudder.

My eyes widened. Oh, God. He was holding a long wooden pole with a glistening dildo at the end, and he'd obviously been fucking her with it.

Zev untied my hands and feet and then he and Wolf lifted the cage off the ground, moving it out of the way. Daisy scooted up beside me, laying her head on the wedge next to mine. We both grinned like blissed-out and satisfied fools, but I knew the guys couldn't be done with us, because they hadn't gotten off yet, either of them, and once Kink Camp started, we'd all be too busy to play much.

I wasn't wrong, because as Zev lay on his side behind me, and Wolf settled in behind Daisy, the wicked gleams in their eyes and the smug grins on their faces said playtime was just getting started . . .

OVATION

Lin Devon

Buttoned to the collar and cinched with a tie. That was Alan Hadrian every weekday from eight a.m. to six p.m. and now, on Saturday date night with his wife, Victoria. At twenty-seven, Alan was young to prefer the modes of old-world elegance, but he had always been his own man. The suits were a little more adventurous on Saturday nights, but suits just the same. Victoria was the effervescent counterpart to his fine vintage. Her auburn hair was swept to one side and gleaming in manicured waves, held back like a curtain to reveal a deceptively shy smile in bright red lipstick. A gilded hair clasp winked its diamond eye beside her sparkling green gaze. But it was the way she looked at him, more than the way she looked, that made them such a stunning pair. He was unashamed to display that he simply couldn't get enough of her.

Victoria, in a thin drape of glittering fabric that drifted weightless around her form, respected that her husband of three years was comfortable being polished, but tonight he seemed a little too constrained. His tailored deep-blue suit was unbuttoned, but he tugged at his collar more than once as they sat in their theater seats. The crowded theater was warm, packed with revelers watching the local stage production of an updated *Great Gatsby*. She knew, though, that it wasn't the body heat that had him straining so hard against his self-imposed tethers.

Victoria's friend Claudia, who had comped them tickets, was resplendent as Daisy Buchanan. As the guileless love interest of the magnanimous Jay Gatsby, she was in her sweet spot, if a little over the top. Her large eyes were made for the stage, and her bouncing enthusiasm contrasted convincingly with her unabashed despondency to form a character that lived every emotion out loud. It wasn't too far a stretch for the very expressive Claudia, but looked impressive to a public eager to be transported. Victoria was deeply proud of her old college roommate.

It was the actor playing Nick Carraway, however, who stole the show. The choice the actor had made to portray Gatsby's friend and narrator as a flawlessly made-up androgynous everyperson added an edgy wit to his lines. In striped shirt and brown wool slacks, a fedora tipped rakishly on his head of waxed black fingerwaves over a face made Hollywood glamorous by vixen makeup, he confused and delighted. He was magnetic. Skin the color of creamy tea was made to look blushing in stage makeup. Full lips gleamed when he spoke; rouged pink gloss made them immediately sensual. Contouring made his bone structure sing, but the smokey haze around bright blue eyes and false lashes made him captivating.

He strolled the stage with easy confidence, and Victoria was enthralled. Masculine build and feminine movement like a dancer, like a cat, he looked ready to pounce or drape that lithe form over a settee. His every line was delivered with subtle notes of innuendo and affection for the lovesick naive. She'd never seen someone so fully inhabit the "It" factor. She glanced at Alan and saw him tug at his collar again. There was tension vibrating through him. His jaw ticked. His chest heaved. His features were soft, but his gaze was electrified in the dark. And his eyes were fixed on just one actor.

Victoria took his hand and Alan kissed her cheek. She took the chance to graze his chin with her fingertips and whisper in his ear, "He's magnificent, isn't he?" She kissed his temple.

Alan met her eyes for a long moment. Lovers in a darkened room, faces close. A stirring energy between them. It could be an innocent question, but wasn't. He knew it. He also knew that the strength of her desires meant she was built to house his wants too. She had proved many times over that the play they shared only made them know each other more deeply. Alan moistened his lips with the tip of his tongue and nodded his agreement. She squeezed his hand, the warm solidity of his knuckles resting on the soft pillow of her thigh.

At intermission, Victoria held her wine in one hand and Alan's hand in the other to lead him to the open air veranda. She took a moment to look at her man in the moonlight and remembered how quickly she'd become interested the first time she'd seen him. Tall and slender and olive skinned with almond eyes, dark hair neatly styled. He was candy in the shape of a man. Her infatuation hadn't dimmed even a little. He smiled down on her and transformed handsome into gorgeous. This wicked grin was magic on her senses.

"Remember that first time on the deck of the river boat?" Her green eyes flared.

He chuckled and slid his hands over her hips to know the contours of her back end. He pressed her against himself, letting her know his memories were just as vivid as hers. "I remember a beautiful girl showing me she wasn't wearing panties under her dress." He tossed an amber lock of hair from her pale shoulder and nuzzled her neck, growling into her ear, "That ass in the moonlight when she leaned over the railing. God, I thought I'd pop right out of my pants."

Victoria held his cheek and guided his mouth to hers, drawing the tip of her tongue across his bottom lip. "She thought she was pulling a fast one, but the wind caught her dress and blew it over her head." They both laughed at the memory. Victoria hooked her fingers into the waistband of his trousers, her thumbs caressing in tandem either side of his fly. "She didn't know who she was flirting with."

"Well, she thought she knew about me, but she sure didn't expect you." His hand drifted upward to graze her breast, his thumb teasing the risen pebble of her nipple through the thin fabric. "You're quite a teammate, sweetheart. I'd never seen anything as beautiful as watching you come on her tongue." He tasted her kiss on an inhale.

"It's been too long." She looked in his eyes to ask what she really wanted to know. "Do you . . . want to go backstage after the show?"

He cast eyes over her face, thinking for a long moment. There was no question whether or not he could confide in her. She was a woman of vast and varied appetites. He wasn't going to shock her. He just needed a moment to appreciate the luck he'd stumbled into having found her. He said, "Yes," into her open mouth, and took her kiss with the passion that had always glued them to each other.

Sitting through the second half of the show, Alan and Victoria were rapt. When Nick Carraway entered the scene Victoria squeezed Alan's thigh, and he laid his fingers loosely over hers. The game was on. No sneaking glances, no shy shrugging. Their choice was made. Alan's beloved crossed her legs to trap his hand between her thighs and curled herself around his arm, her head resting on his shoulder. He understood. It was like watching the evening's sirloin stroll around the dinner table wagging and wobbling and just out of reach. It made him feel ravenous. He tugged at his collar.

Backstage was a madhouse of theater people, cast and crew, invited guests tossing congratulations and pouring champagne. The toasts were many and the mood celebratory. After the riot of applause they'd received, they knew what a stellar job they'd done. Claudia was swimming in accolades. She engaged in a short conversation with Victoria and Alan, but left them to make her rounds. They didn't mind. She could be a bit much, needing so much continual and repeated praise. Besides, they were both on the lookout for someone else. So when an arm was thrown over each of their shoulders, they were delighted to see that the actor who'd smashed the show with his interpretation of Nick Carraway was grinning between them.

"I feel amazing." He laughed.

Alan slipped an arm around his waist to hold him in place. "You were amazing."

He exaggerated a pout. "Past tense already?"

Alan laughed. This was an ego he could praise. "You *are* amazing."

He lingered too long on Alan's face and made him blush. "No, you are." His eyes searched Alan's, a question unspoken and silently answered between them.

Alan sucked his lower lip in the way that always drove Victoria wild and said, "I'm Alan. This is my wife, Victoria. May we know the name of the brightest star in this little community constellation?"

He grinned at Alan and turned his head to cast his bright smile on Victoria. "Bryn. My name is Bryn."

She laid a hand on his wrist slung over her shoulder and slipped down to grasp his fingers. *"Enchanté."*

Up close he was stunning under the stage makeup, now sweated away at the temples. Trapped under his arm, Victoria was quickly drunk on the scent of his exertion, a heady mix of male sweat and faded perfume. It was humid this close to him fresh from the stage lights.

He hummed against her ear, "Enchanted, are you?" He turned his face to Alan. "The sentiment is . . . mutual?"

Alan's fingers tightened on Bryn's narrow waist. "Painfully so."

Bryn chuckled softly and sucked in a deep breath as if to cool the building heat. "Ay me, what gifts nobles lay at a pauper's feet."

Alan laughed. "What givers receive is a gift indeed. Twofold returned for a prince who thinks himself a pauper. Can we see your dressing room?"

Victoria marveled at her husband's ability to get to the point with haste and elegance. Bryn smiled down at Victoria's lifted eyebrow. "You tease me."

"Fair exchange for what you've done to us all evening. But no, teasing is not on the menu," Victoria purred.

"Oh, there's a menu, is there?" Bryn was cheeky, but he was toying his teeth with his tongue, intrigued. "Care to tell me the main course?"

Alan swept a hand down the buttons of Bryn's shirt, coming to rest on his taut belly. "If you're very hungry, there are three."

Bryn's face was openly beaming. He cleared his throat and took them both by the hand marveling, "Sounds fucking delicious," as he led them down the hall.

It was a shared dressing room, of course. A little theater like this didn't have private accommodations, even for someone as

firmly seated in star position as Bryn. But the room was merci-
fully empty. He led them in and gestured with one graceful arm.
"Our salon, my dears."

He leaned on the interior doorknob as his guests stepped
inside. The space was crowded with racks of costumes, lined on
one side with lockers and the other with a row of lighted vanity
tables. It felt like a closet.

"Just as charming as you suspected, I'm sure," Bryn said
deprecatingly. A short couch and a matching chair occupied the
center of the space, a squat coffee table between them. "May I
offer you a seat?"

"I brought my own," Victoria delivered with a wink.

The men stood side by side and watched as Victoria leaned
on one of the vanities to fix her hair in the mirror. The slinky
drape of her dress, held aloft with angel-hair straps, drifted
around her body, hugging only at the deadliest curves, of which
she had many. With her leaning this way the drape fell forward
and exposed her naked form down to the navel and back again.
She swiveled to peek at her audience and saw her effect on their
new friend's face. If flirtation is chess then she was the queen.
She smiled at them, shrugged, and paid no mind to her shoulder strap tumbling to her elbow. One gleaming teardrop breast
dropped like a soundless bomb into the middle of their little
game and jiggled. Victoria casually lifted the hem of her short
dress and sat her bottom on the tabletop.

Bryn cleared his throat and croaked, "You seem to have lost
your modesty panel, Victoria."

Alan loosened his tie and Bryn unfastened his top button in
tandem with each other, though neither looked anywhere but at
her. She pulled a pink rose from the arrangement beside her and
held it to her nose. She plucked a petal and placed it like a little
cap on the toasted circle of her areola. "Better?"

Bryn nodded and said, "No. I've never in my life wanted more for a breeze in a closed room."

Alan laughed. He took the door from Bryn's grip, gently closing it behind him. "Now it's a closed room."

Bryn's eyes bounced from Alan to Victoria, the glaze over his irises belying his calm. He was just as close to the edge as they were. But Alan knew how to guide his intended. He stepped closer to Bryn, his chest a scant inch from the other's and craned his neck to plant a single chaste kiss at the corner of Bryn's jaw. He inhaled beside Bryn's ear and placed a gentle hand on his chest.

"You are magnificent," he said, and pressed himself bodily forward.

The air escaped Bryn's lungs under the crush of a need-hard body hot in his grip. Alan's fly strained to conceal him, but this close Bryn was made unmistakably aware of the heavy line of flesh ticking against his hip. Alan had him pinned bodily, but Victoria held those eyes. As he watched her over Alan's shoulder, she blew a stream of cool air down her chest and the petal lifted off like a butterfly.

Alan growled against Bryn's neck and opened his mouth like a vampire over his pulse, hot tongue licking. He said, "All night long she's just been starving for your kiss."

Bryn's eyes rolled back momentarily and he clutched at Alan's hips. He said, "Well, we can't have her starving."

Alan smiled, bit his own lip and then Bryn's, but gently. "We wouldn't want anyone to starve."

Bryn marveled at the two playful creatures he'd somehow caught. Or had caught him. They were so much in answer to the prayers he'd made in the depths of wettest dreamland he almost couldn't believe they were real. To seduce and be seduced by an adoring public, to reap the benefits of real sexual magnetism, it was the final confirmation he had what it took. A dream of Hollywood blossomed in his imagination.

He said to Alan, "I can't tell you how happy I am that you came tonight."

Alan grinned, "Mm, not yet. Besides"—he grazed Bryn's shoulder with his teeth—"you first."

Bryn chuckled against Alan's open mouth and sank into him when Alan closed the distance. The sight of this beautiful man polished to gleaming now reduced to wanton desires was an aphrodisiac. He was caged thunder in Bryn's hands. His heartbeat hammered in his chest and reverberated straight through Bryn's clothes. That Bryn had done this to him by the simple trick of his stage prowess was the highest compliment. This was the praise he craved. To be irresistible, to bring a man like this to the edge of his confines, to be begged for the gift of his body. He would have them both on their knees.

Bryn tasted Alan's tongue with his own, lips fastened to contain the jungle heat between them. Alan's hands roamed Bryn's body, eager to know his shape, to have every part in his memory. His hands found Bryn's fly and caressed there with a knowing palm, the length of him swelling. Bryn let out a low moan when Alan squeezed, cupped him at the crux, and slid along his length. The ridge of his head clearly delineated in the fabric made Alan's mouth water. Certainly, it had been too long.

Bryn watched Victoria watching him. She was a lioness waiting for her opportunity. She was starving, Alan had said, starving for him. She breathed with her lips parted, fingers clutching the edge of the vanity, eyes sparkling in her beautiful face. That one neglected breast peeked at him, playful, delicious. She was glamorous in Bryn's mind, the epitome of sexual grace. Soft curves and flesh that yielded. Long, lithe thighs, body soft as pillows, and the tense wet grip of the sheath hidden in her belly. She scented his thoughts while Alan seasoned his body.

Alan turned to Victoria and held out his hand. "Come, darling. Come here."

Bryn gestured his agreement with an open hand for her, but couldn't speak. Alan was unbuttoning his shirt, sucking the sweat from his throat, and dancing his cock against Bryn's in hard, grinding circles.

The sight of these two men wound so tight around each other now reaching out for her was all the wine she'd ever need. Victoria sauntered across the scant distance, acutely aware of the subtle movements of her body in her dress. Every inch was erogenous. As she came she let her other strap fall, her dress now a shimmering skirt slung low on her hips. She was enfolded into the sauna heat between her Alan and their Bryn. The men crossed at the forearm to hold her close around the waist.

Alan sucked Bryn's earlobe, then Victoria's neck, as she pressed her lips to Bryn's kiss. He was delightfully sweet, lips soft as a woman's against hers. His seeking tongue tasted of champagne and chocolate truffles and she thought he was guilt-free indulgence personified. Bryn's hand drifted up her back to hold her behind the neck and keep her steady as he deepened their kiss. Alan's hand drifted lower to find her plump bottom beneath the fabric and squeeze. Those deft fingers massaged so close to center she sang an involuntary note into Bryn's mouth. But she and Alan had all night, the rest of their lives together. This moment with Bryn was fleeting. After all, the door had no lock.

Victoria's hands were talented. She had his trousers unzipped before he noticed what she was doing. She was never one for half measures. His body jerked on a gasp as she found him inside his fly and encircled his cock against her palm. He broke their kiss to suck breath as her hand danced along his shaft.

Alan took his advantage when Bryn nuzzled his cheek against him. Their mouths met and tangled without a second thought. Under Alan's power Bryn was lost to sensation. After the subtle rasp of Alan's chin against his own, tongue delving the confines of Bryn's mouth, he was almost completely undone when Alan's hand met Victoria's and together they pulled his cock into the open air.

Alan bent to kiss Victoria's clavicle, and never ceased his insistent stroke as he dipped his head to suck Victoria's beaded nipples. He was first to fall. All his composed and polished facade crumbled in the face of his own primal hunger. He was on his knees. One hand held Bryn to the door with a forearm across his belly, while the other squeezed his dick in tugging rhythmic pulses.

Victoria cast her eyes on the sight of him, her beloved crouched at the monolith, fist cinched around Bryn's pretty cock and stroking. She met Alan's eyes, bright with wonder, as he parted his lips and bathed the swollen head of Bryn's cock with his tongue. Bryn uttered a subtle curse and leaned his head back against the door. He didn't see Victoria join her partner, but felt her slide from his grip.

She met her husband's eyes over the gift between them. She and he together met mouths around the intrusion of Bryn's pulsing head. In tandem they slathered the length of him. Bryn, caught in the center of their kiss, heaved breath with his eyes squeezed shut. But he wanted to be housed, and deeply. He found the straining curve of a stubbled jaw and guided his girth into the confines of Alan's sucking mouth. He held Alan's face, covering his ears to seat himself deeper. Alan was a talented man. He closed his eyes, sinking into sensory deprivation. Without sound and sight he was a vessel designed for taste, touch, and scent. He housed Bryn as he was urged. Completely. Bryn mumbled something poetic and complimentary before pulling free, only to have Victoria draw him swiftly back to know the hot, wet welcome of her own lips, her tongue, her throat.

He was gentler with her, some ingrained manner toward women. But Victoria would not be coddled. She slid her fingertips into his pockets to rock him forward, show him what talent they both possessed. Bryn whimpered an oath on a ragged breath, too close. She met her husband's eye. Should they let him up? No. Alan took Bryn's balls in hand and tugged them gently, his thumb arcing across sensitive flesh with knowing tenderness. Victoria stroked his shaft like silk over steel, marveling at the crystal bead of lubrication formed at the tip. Bryn found the back of either neck and guided their mouths together again around him. He held them there, like a steam press as he pumped his hips and slid his erection between them.

He didn't want to stop, but Victoria slid a curious hand up the back of his leg and found his center hidden inside clothes and between muscular cheeks. She pressed flesh with the tips of her fingers, felt him yield and go rigid. He garbled a moan and brought their two mouths to his raging cock head to flick him with their tongues and suckle him with their greedy lips, urging all the while without words for him to come.

He came.

In a rush his body filled with white hot magma and overflowed in a gushing wave. It cascaded from him in pulses, too long overdue, tearing through his thoughts, scorching whole valleys from his mind. He was a star in their spotlight. He could do anything. He would do everything. Their shared hunger for him was as intoxicating as any standing ovation. And they were hungry for him. They didn't miss a drop.

Bryn's legs failed him and he slid down the door to join them on the floor. They drew him close, covering his face in kisses.

He was suddenly bone tired. The evening's excesses of food and drink and bodily pleasure had taxed him flat.

He was sucking breath but managed, "You've sapped me dry, little vampires."

Alan kissed him at the corner of his mouth. "We wouldn't take anything from you we wouldn't happily give back. But someone's been knocking on that door for the last three or four minutes."

Bryn's eyes snapped open and he was on his feet like he'd been electrified. Victoria and Alan were pristine but for a little sweat on the upper lip when they opened the door and saw a small group of cast members standing there looking to change out of their stage costumes. Alan and Victoria apologized, proclaiming some mishap with Victoria's dress that needed fixing.

"You can always count on an actor to know how to sew things up." Victoria winked at Bryn.

The group's eyes shifted collectively to Bryn, who leaned on the edge of a vanity and shrugged, looking worlds more disheveled than his guests. His fly was undone.

"We'll be waiting for your next performance, Bryn," Alan said.

"Just let us know the time and place," Victoria added.

The horde of them rushed inside as Alan and Victoria squeezed out. Sated, but not yet fully satisfied, the young couple exited the scene together. They strode down the hall hand in hand, triumphant, and lifted by the sound of bawdy laughter and riotous applause behind them.

ONCE MORE
UNTO THE
BREACH

Kelvin Sparks

Xan doesn't dream like he used to. Maybe that's for the best. Back on Earth, he dreamed too much, too vividly, too darkly, always finding himself pulled away, covered in a sheen of sweat. Out here though, on the verge of habited space, he finds his dreams are quiet. They're always the same too: the sensation of lying on something endless, floating weightless in nothing. It's peaceful and dark and quiet, in a way that makes Xan wonder if it's induced by station management when he's more lucid. (He only wonders for a split second, before he realizes it's a question he'd rather not have answered.)

Induced or not, it makes it easier to wake and pull himself out of bed and into consciousness as quickly as possible when the alarm for his shift blares. And it does just that as he's pulled into the waking world now: a low but constant labored hum, soft warm light—just close enough to a real sunrise to remind Xan of home, and just short enough that he misses it—spreading over the room. Next to his bunk, a small silver watch—one of the few things he brought with him to the station—shows UTC 02:27. One hour and thirty-three minutes until his shift is meant to start. Which can only mean one thing.

Juno's voice crackles a little over the radio. "Rise and shine. Guess who's been put on cover duty."

Xan groans, reaching for the plastic box of caffeine pills next to his watch. He swallows them dry, because even though he knows it's dangerous, he also knows how expensive it is to ship water out this far. "Why did it have to be us?"

She laughs, and it makes a little bit of Xan's heart lift, even if a little bit of the laughter turns to static. "Because we're good, Xan . . . . Well, that and we're the only people on the station who've had enough bed rest to be cleared for the Jump."

There are few things that Xan loves about life on Station 028. There are few things *to* love. It's a dark series of titanium and Kevlar boxes, half nailed down to each other and to the asteroid below. His cabin is a little bigger than anything he could afford back on Earth, at least, but it's still barely seventy square feet. Corporate insurance covers his hormones—and even his top surgery last time he was planet-side—but getting medical supplies delivered is so difficult he sometimes wonders *when* (not if) he'll run out of needles. The station is far enough from the core of the Sol System that it's easy to forget home even exists, and it only seems to drift a little further away each day.

But he loves the Jump. He loves it more than he has ever loved anything before. He loves it because, more than anything else, it makes him feel alive. Not just alive for him, but for Juno too. *As* Juno too.

"Five minutes?" he says, and he can feel his heart start to pound with all the excitement and terror in the galaxy all at once. "And I'll meet you at the docking bay?"

Juno is there to meet him, in the same gray-green boiler suit as always, the one that clings to her round hips and the soft curve of her belly. Her dark, curly hair is pulled back into a low ponytail, a few strands loose around her forehead, and Xan knows that by the end of their Jump, those hairs will be stuck to her forehead with sweat. She smiles when she sees him, wide and warm in a way that makes the dim fluorescent lighting seem a little brighter.

"Ready?" she asks. Behind her, their mech stands, engines ready and purring. It's small, as mechs go, although that's not saying a huge amount. It's around ten meters tall, all faded yellow metal and covered in scuff marks, and whenever Xan looks at it, he's always struck by how much it reminds him of some kind of insect: a round cockpit on top of four evenly spaced digitigrade legs, a mining drill at their center.

"Are we ever?" he replies.

It doesn't feel as dramatic any more, that moment when he and his copilot and the mech become one. The first time Xan Jumped with somebody, the feeling of it—the slow slip of a sense of where he ended and everything else began—scared him so much that he pulled the connection. But that was worse—both the nausea at being violently shoved back into his own body and having the cost of a failed Jump taken from his wages that month—so Xan never did it a second time. He got used to it. With Juno as his copilot, he even started to like it: him becoming her, her becoming him, them both becoming something more than themselves, all steel and 2219-T6 aluminum alloy.

I'm here. Juno doesn't quite so much say or think it as feel it, and Xan feels it as part of her too. *I've got you.*

Their breathing is heavy, and it gets heavier still as the mech moves from the docking bay into the hangar. When the hangar doors open—silently, and Xan will never get used to the silence of space—both their bodies hold their breath for a moment. Xan doesn't *see* the asteroid beneath them because he doesn't really see anything, but he can *sense* it's there. And he can sense the breach in the asteroid's surface too, an impossibly wide, impossible dark fissure in rock.

We good to drop? he thinks, even though he can feel Juno's answer before he even thinks the question. She doesn't think or feel anything particular in response, but their mech moves forward, beginning its long, slow, steady descent into pitch black.

The shift goes by quickly. At least, it does for Xan; the six hours—and then the extra hour and twenty minutes—melt away to nothing. But it goes by slowly as well, as though there'll be no end to this *being* between the two of them, everything slow and all at once simultaneously. It probably passes slower for Juno, with every cell of her gray matter focused on making the mech—*their body*—move, using its legs and drill to pull cobalt from stone-buried veins. She's the one who makes this whole venture profitable; he's the one who keeps them alive while they do it, makes sure the engines stay running and the life support is on, keeps track of their oxygen levels and the state of their radiation shielding.

He can feel his own heartbeat, even though he's not in his own body. He can feel Juno's too—solid and steady, growing a little faster each time she remembers that he's inside of her. And the mech doesn't have a heartbeat, but he can feel the closest thing it has to one, the steady movement of the engine's turbines. And—as the mech, as the two of them together—he can sense their warm, fragile little bodies inside of their greater self.

Keep me safe, Juno feels, and there's a flash of something alongside it, an image of *home*, of somewhere green and calm, solid ground under their feet, bright smiles on the faces of people that Xan doesn't recognize but—because of Juno—he *knows.* This is what "safe" means to her, a little piece of herself that she shares with him, and if he had a body right now Xan wonders if he might weep at the fact that she trusts him enough to share it, and then weep still that she trusts him enough to give him responsibility for her body.

What a joy it is to have so much control over someone else's body. What a privilege. What a burden. He takes care of Juno in other ways—does her antiandrogen injections when she asks, makes sure she remembers to change her estrogen patches, despite the irregular hours they work—but nothing compares to *this*. Her body twitches, and he feels it next to his body and inside her body and through the sensors in the cockpit all at once.

On paper, they've only known each other for a few months, only met for the first time after they shipped out here, to the edge of the known galaxy. But it feels like they have known each other forever, like they have been at each other's sides for a whole lifetime. Perhaps they have. After all, right now Xan *is* Juno, and she *is* him. And when this shift ends and they both eject from the Jump, becoming their own selves once more, they will still remember everything.

It's an old joke at this point that Jump partners inevitably end up sleeping with each other. It was an old joke back when the first few pairs of people Jumped, back when the only mechs piloted like that were for war. It made a little more sense back then, Xan thinks. The intimacy of becoming the same being for a bit, the adrenaline rush of battle, the relief of surviving. The two of them—together and separately—have never experienced the chaos of battle, nor come back so relieved to have survived that they don't know what else to do but fuck. Instead, they have the slow, lonely push to pull as much valuable material from the breach in the asteroid's surface as possible.

That, and they have each other.

Xan doesn't *know* he'll fuck Juno in their post-shift communal shower before he goes in. Juno doesn't either—Xan knows because he *was* her just moments ago. But when they make it there—boiler suits and thermal layers strewn carelessly over the changing bench—it feels like an inevitability. Just as the Jump is disorienting to begin with, so is leaving the Jump. When Xan holds a hand in front of his face, his fingers shake a little, but he barely feels it; it's indescribably odd to have only a single body again. He would say it feels like a dream—not quite real—but in truth it's worse than that, dull and muted where dreams are bright and vivid. He feels not quite alive again yet. He feels like just one half of a whole. And he can't really be that whole again—not until their next Jump at least—but he can try the next closest thing.

Juno kisses him first, like she knows exactly what he's thinking. She probably does. They stand under neighboring showerheads, desperate to be as close as they can, neither having quite the courage to touch until Juno reaches over. She clasps a hand over Xan's shoulder—stills for a moment to remember what it feels like to have skin on skin—and tugs him forward. Their mouths don't quite line up because Juno is a little taller than he is, but their faces are still close enough together that Xan can feel her warm breath on his lips. Her shower is a hotter temperature than his, a perfect steady rain, and as the room fills with steam it's easy to forget that there is anywhere in the universe other than here.

When she kisses him, it's soft and closed mouthed, the hand that's not on his shoulder gently stroking his wet hair. It's perfect, exactly how Xan loves to be kissed, just how Juno has always kissed him, and with the little part of his brain that's cogent Xan wonders which memory Juno knows to kiss him like this from. Maybe it was his first, when he was newly

eighteen and drunk for the first time. Perhaps it was the first kiss
he had as a man, twenty-four years old and with a girlfriend
he'd had long enough that he trusted her to know that she knew
exactly how to kiss him. It broke his heart when she left. Perhaps it's both, or neither, or something else entirely. Whatever
it is, Juno kisses him perfectly, and even though it's soft and . . .
well, not quite *chaste*, but as close as the two of them can get,
he wants to press his body up against hers.

"You should turn your shower off if we're doing this," Juno
says, when they finally part for air. "Management will get pissed
if they find out we're wasting water like that."

Fucking while just one shower is on will still waste water,
but Xan doesn't see a point to arguing. He does as she says.
When he returns to Juno, he takes the lead this time. He grabs
her hip with one hand, gently turns her so her back is to him,
and touches her, his fingertips gently stroking the curve of her
shoulder blades, just the way she likes it.

She's never told him how to touch her, but he knows. He
knows how it feels, remembers what it was like the first time
somebody touched her like this. It's not quite a whole experience—just little fragments—but he remembers it all the same;
the man with the kind brown eyes, soft purple lights and a window that looked down onto the spaceship drydock. He remembers the smell, sage and ginger and eucalyptus—*a scented candle? Incense maybe? No, in a shipyard cabin, it would have had
to be a diffuser because of the rules against open flames*—and
the way that man touched Juno's bare back as she lay in bed,
watching the ships go by. Soft, slow strokes to start with, along
the length of her back and just with fingertips. And then the heel
of the hand, a slow continuous movement, fluid as the oil on his
palms. Xan doesn't have oil to hand, but he touches Juno all the
same. She tenses and then relaxes, tendons and muscles reacting

just the way Xan remembers feeling them react when he was her, melts into his touch. Her head is turned over her shoulder, so Xan can see it when her eyelids flutter shut and she lets something that sounds suspiciously like a muffled moan gently push its way out from between her lips.

"You can do more than this to me if you want," she says, somewhere between a promise and a request, a knowing smile pulling at one corner of her lips. From that smile, Xan knows she's remembering something in particular.

"You'll have to be more specific." He smiles back, although as with everything he feels it like it's from a distance, a kind of muffled sensation, like he's not quite in his body still. "There are a lot of things I could do."

Juno's cheeks are already flushed from the heat of the water, but the color becomes a little pinker as she turns to face him. Even with the distance from his body, Xan can feel her breath on his lips, heavy and hot as the heartbeat he can feel in his hands. She reaches out to him, cups a hand gently around his jaw and cheeks, and just that little touch makes everything feel more solid and real.

"Do you remember that time?" she begins, even though she knows that he must remember, or else she wouldn't. "When we—*you* were working on that freighter passing through the Kuiper belt. She was a mechanic, I think. Maybe an engineer. She had deep-set eyes and blue hair with the roots just showing. Smelled of tobacco and vanilla."

Xan does remember. He remembers everything that Juno does and more. He remembers the dim lighting in the cabin— not because the two of them wanted mood lighting, but because the freighter was in the last week of its run and running low on fuel—and the way that woman had kissed him, not with softness like Juno but hungrily, with an open mouth and her teeth on Xan's bottom lip. He remembers how he'd fucked her, bent her over the edge of the bunk and stroked her cock as he'd pushed his own harnessed cock inside her.

"I don't have them with me," he finds himself saying, before he even thinks the words through. "My harness or my cock. I can't do that."

"No. But you have hands." As if to prove a point, Juno moves her own hand from his cheek, moves down Xan's body with a single smooth, slow stroke, until it meets his, her fingers gently splayed over the back of his palm. "You can touch me like that. I *want* you to touch me like that."

Xan's body is pressed against Juno's when he reaches down to her cock, flushed skin on flushed skin, the raised scars on his chest gently brushing against the soft new curves of hers. She's soft in his cupped hand, but Xan knows that doesn't mean anything. Even if he didn't know it, Juno would be making it clear with the sounds that come from her. They start with a hitched breath as he begins, firm pressure in his palm as he gently, slowly strokes her. Then they become something else— a moan, but far louder and braver than the one before. Xan's face is pressed into the crook of Juno's neck, trailing kisses down onto her shoulder, so he doesn't see the look on her face when she lets it out, but *fuck* does he wish he had. He wishes it more than anything.

Xan knows that this can't last. Once this asteroid is stripped to the bare bones and Station 028 tagged for redeployment, the two of them could be sent on jobs at opposite ends of the galaxy. He knows that even though Juno knows him more deeply than anyone has before, it's only been a few months since they met. But with Juno in his arms and her cock in his hand, it's easy to forget, or at least to let himself pretend to forget. He presses down on her more than strokes, steady and even, although his thumb dips to circle the head and when she moans again he can't help but do the same against her neck.

Juno's whole body shakes when she comes, pressing up against Xan's even more tightly than it was before. *God*, that's Xan's favorite thing about fucking—seeing and feeling and hearing somebody come undone and knowing that he was the one who did it. And when it's Juno, it's even better, because Xan knows he did it exactly how she wanted him to.

Xan pulls away from Juno's neck to look her in the eye, and even with the shower still on, her face is covered with a sheen of sweat and her breath heavy. She smiles at him, still out of breath but broad and warm. Xan tries to ignore the little ache in his chest at the sight. Instead, he leans forward, and presses a soft kiss to her forehead.

"After the next shift," Juno says, eventually, "*I* want to touch *you*."

ONLY PROP
WEAPONS
ALLOWED

Melanie Anton

"Bend over so I can zip you all the way up."

"Ugh, I can't touch my toes anymore."

For all the silly and wonderful ways that Craig still moves me, he can be a royal pain in my ass when it comes to change. He doesn't like it and does everything he can to avoid it. You'd think that, by fifty, he'd have figured out that life is nothing but change, but no. So, when I suggested he retire his Superman cosplay (I swear it's old enough to go to college), naturally he threw a full-scale fit.

"I can still fit into it."

"No, you can't, babe. It's okay. Take it off."

I knew he'd fuss and whine (and here's where I roll my eyes) but in the end, he'd agree with me that he could no longer wear his old Superman cosplay. Time had marched on, and we were no longer the spry twenty-somethings of our local comic con. Surprisingly enough, I took my age in stride, allowing the softness, gentle lines, and gray hair to do what they wanted. Craig was fighting it every step of the way. A military man to the core, retirement at fifty did not suit him well. It felt like a fire had gone out in him. A loss of passion. I was certainly feeling that loss in the bedroom.

Was I hitting my stride just as he was losing his? It looked like that was a distinct possibility. I knew we needed a change and so I hatched a plan to try and rekindle some of the old flame. I was taking him to the same comic convention we had met at back in 1995, but he didn't know it yet. Hence my having him try on his old Superman cosplay.

I gave him a hug, gently running my hands up and down his back that had carried rucksacks across deserts and lifted heavy artillery onto vehicles headed into potentially life-threatening situations. Yet he always came home. To me. Our marriage couldn't just fizzle out like this after all we have been through together. I wouldn't allow it. We could reignite the passion. I knew we could. At least, I hoped we could.

"It's okay. I love you, and your body is hotter to me today than it was the day we met."

He chuckled, kissed the top of my head, and went into his home office, shutting me out. Again. Damn. I turned and went into the art studio, gently closing the door behind me. Two could play this game, but it was a game I had swiftly grown tired of playing. I turned on the computer, did some searches, and found what I was looking for on a costuming website. I cringed a bit at the total but hit that enter button like I was deploying a missile. Yeah, a missile right at our marriage if I wasn't careful.

A week later a large box arrived on our doorstep.

"What did you order?"

"Open it and see for yourself."

Craig cut open the box and pulled apart a plastic bag to reveal a green spandex unitard and a bright red wig.

"Oh, those are mine." I grabbed at the items. "Yours must be on the bottom."

I bit my lip and hoped he would try to take this in stride as he pulled out a dark gray spandex and rubber suit with black accents. The frown he wore did not bode well for success, but I pushed on.

"Remember how exciting the comic cons were in our twenties and thirties?" I circled him while he stood there silently. I wondered what he was thinking. Was he remembering the fun we'd had with friends? The after-hours hotel parties? Or possibly our enthusiastic lovemaking that sent the hotel guests on both sides banging on our walls to shut up?

He looked at the cosplay that he held in his hands, then looked at me.

"You want me to be the Bat to your . . . ?" He nodded toward what I held in my hands.

"Ivy."

"Right. Poisonous, if I remember correctly." He chuckled.

At that point I felt braver, as if his small laugh had loosened something coiled tightly in my chest, squeezing my heart. Clutching my costume tightly against me, I touched his arm with my free hand.

"Please go try it on. For me. For us."

He looked confused for a moment. I don't think he caught on that this was about our relationship, but he would.

"Sure, but only if you try on yours too."

To say I bolted from the room to try on my Poison Ivy was an understatement. I was fully invested in this endeavor. I just hoped that he would feel the same at some point.

I changed into my new costume with as much speed as skintight spandex, and my protesting joints, allowed. I shrugged the bright red wig over my graying hair and looked in the mirror. Yeah, there was quite a bit more of me to love, and my face had softened somewhat, but she was still there. That fiery, outspoken, funny, and determined woman was still alive and ready for more adventure. The costume fit me perfectly, hugging every curve. I felt buoyed by the tightness of the fabric and made my way across the bedroom with a bit more strut, a bit more sass. I blew myself a kiss in the mirror and walked back into the kitchen.

A minute later, Craig came out of his office. Damn! He looked delicious. Seriously. Edible. Everything about the costume was perfect and fit him like he was born to wear it. He looked like Batman, and the sight of my personal superhero turned me on.

"Okay. This is actually really cool. It feels good and it fits great. You made an excellent choice. I even feel a bit different." He pulled me close, bent down, and looked me in the eye. "You look amazing as well, but I know you didn't do this just so we could admire each other. So what gives?"

I stepped back and pulled some papers out of the drawer. "Next weekend is WonderCon, up in Anaheim. I bought two weekend passes and booked us a suite at the Hilton. I thought that . . . "—doubt crept into my voice—"it would be nice to get away from our mundane lives for a bit, reconnect, and play, even if only for this weekend, like we used to do."

He took the papers from my hand, put them on the counter, and pulled me toward him. Firmly tucked against his chest, I could hear his heart beating, reassuring me that everything would be alright and that I was safe. In that moment, I didn't want to feel safe. I wanted to be bold. So I swallowed my nervousness and said everything that I had been missing about our relationship. How he barely touched me sexually and that, though we got along splendidly most of the time, our romantic and sexual intimacy had waned drastically in the past five years. How I saw this as an opportunity to rekindle the flame of who we once were, together. I might have shed a few tears as I unburdened myself, but I did my best to not let him see.

Craig sighed, kissed the top of my head, and tightened his arms around me. "Let's do it." A man of few words, but those were all the words I needed at that moment. I'd take it!

WonderCon weekend was finally here. We checked into our hotel room, unpacked, and went to the hotel bar for a drink and a light dinner. We met up with friends we hadn't seen in years and one drink became several. It was nice to see Craig loosening up and having fun. I felt hopeful for the first time in a long time.

Everything got kind of fuzzy after that, but I remember Craig and I leaning on each other and giggling like teenagers as we rode the elevator to our floor. We got undressed and crawled gratefully into the luxurious king-size bed. Shortly after, we both fell asleep. My last glance at the glowing face of my phone told me that it was only 9:30. So much for reliving our glory days! At this age, all-nighters just don't happen without serious repercussions for the next couple days. Thank goodness we have a bit more sense than that.

After a bit of a slow morning, we got up and got ready for a full Saturday of, hopefully, mischief and mayhem. Still no luck on sexy time, but Craig was more attentive than usual. He smiled and cast several appreciative glances my way, after I was all dressed up. To be honest, he looked amazing. I wondered if I should have cosplayed as a pirate so that I'd be able to "raid" his "booty" later. Still, I think we looked quite impressive as Batman and Poison Ivy. We sauntered through the hotel lobby and into the convention arm in arm. We were off to play!

Now, every good soldier has a battle plan, and in my years of marriage to a military man, I had learned a trick or two. Since I knew that he was now "mostly" on board, I could set about wooing him in a way that I hoped he couldn't—wouldn't —resist. I had long ago utilized the art of the tease to capture his attention. I set about doing the same, right in the halls of the convention, surrounded by thousands of people bent on doing one thing—having fun!

My cosplay clung to my ample ass like a second skin and every time I bent over to "adjust" something (let's be honest, I did it for the looks), someone was scoping out my backside. I always made sure to catch their eye and give them a little half smile before I turned to Craig, tossed my magnificent red mane of faux hair over my shoulder, and looked at him while I licked my lips. As the day wore on, I noticed him getting frustrated and mildly uncomfortable.

We attended a panel called "Cosplayers of a Certain Age" and I spent most of my time with one hand crawling up Craig's thigh while I looked straight ahead. I couldn't tell you what the panelists said; I was too hyper-focused on the sexy man next to me. I was already warm to begin with, thanks to perimeno-pause, but this was a whole different kind of heat. The heat that starts in your crotch and moves slowly, spreading out from your center, suffusing your limbs with a weighted heat that made me want to lay back and spread my thighs for the next human ani-mal to consume. I was getting horny as fuck, just sitting there with my hand inching slowly up my husband's thigh.

Craig grabbed my hand right before I reached the promised land, brought it to his lips and kissed the back of it, then turned it over and bit the pad below my thumb. "Behave" was all I heard as his mouth brushed my ear. He then placed my hand back in my lap. It was working. I was getting to him.

In a surprise turn of events, he ordered lunch and took me to a park across from the convention center. We ate in silence for a bit before he turned to me and spoke.

"I know what you're trying to do, Kat, but I don't know if it will do any good." My heart plummeted to my fancy shoes, and I waited in growing dread over what he might say next. "I feel so useless. What am I now? Who am I now? I'm retired, washed up, body changing, and worried that I'm no longer the man you want. I love you so much, but I'm embarrassed. I don't think I could handle it if you turned away from me." He fell silent and looked down at his sandwich.

That was a lot to unpack, and he was so off-base regarding my feelings for him that I almost laughed. But I didn't. Here we were, both unsure of ourselves, and each other, both afraid to speak on it until there was no other option. All I could do was tell him how I felt and then back up those words with actions.

I put my hand under his chin and made him look at me. "I love you so much. You are beautiful to me. Even more beautiful, if that were fucking possible. You are not useless. You just haven't found your new purpose, your new direction, yet. Give it a bit of time. This whole retirement thing is new to both of us. We'll find a new normal. Your op tempo was so high the last five years that I'm sure this new life feels like some sort of letdown to you." I let go of his chin and sat back, hesitant of what my next words might bring. "But I'll be honest with you, the last five years have been rough on me. You were hardly ever home and, when you were, you barely touched me. I felt like we were roommates, and I still feel that way." A couple tears fell from my face onto my sandwich. I set it down. I detest soggy bread.

Craig's face went still with my words, and I could see that he was thinking, hard. A small smile grew until he was laughing. "This whole time I thought you didn't want me, and here you were, thinking I didn't want you!" He pulled me close and kissed me softly, his tongue lightly, hesitantly, seeking mine. I melted into his embrace and slid my tongue across his, letting out a gentle moan. Oh, how I had missed this.

After that, he quickly figured out why I had planned this weekend. I reminded him of a teasing game we used to play with each other at conventions and his eyes lit up at the memories. We walked back across the street and dumped our picnic. He turned to me, nodded once, bowed, kissed my hand, and strode into the convention, leaving me standing outside, counting to fifty. It was all part of the familiar game we had wordlessly agreed to play.

There's only so much you can do sexually while in public and fully encased in spandex and rubber. He'd catch me as I came out of the bathroom, push me up against the wall, and run his hands across my breasts. I'd pass him in one of the halls and cop a feel of his cock (albeit through his dance belt and spandex suit) before swiftly walking on. He'd stalk me. I'd escape, only to find him waiting for me, grabbing me, and pushing me into an empty room where he'd hold my wrists behind my back as he kissed me with a ferocity he hasn't shown in well over a decade. I'd bite his lip in response.

"Fuck," he whispered.

"Later," I replied, escaping his grasp and, swaying my hips, sauntered out the door and straight into a security guard. Giggling like a teenager, I waved to the guard and strolled away.

I don't know which one of us was winning the game, but I didn't care. The rules weren't the same this time around, and I was no longer keeping score. We kept up the teasing, and the shenanigans, all day, enjoying a colorful riot of heat and glorious fun.

By the time all the panels were over, and the vendor hall

was shut down for the night, we were both so keyed up that we didn't make it to our hotel room. Craig pulled me into an alcove on our hotel floor and pushed me between the side of the ice machine and the wall.

"How much do you care about these?" he asked, pointing to our cosplay.

"I don't" was all I was able to get out before he pulled out a bat-shaped throwing star and proceeded to cut my cosplay off me.

There are several things I trust Craig with implicitly. His ability to use any weapon accurately and effectively was one of them. I barely twitched as he expertly cut my green spandex, vines, and flowers away from my body until I stood there in my green underwear and bra. Even my fancy shoes were sacrificed to the wicked man wielding the bat blade. Having done its work, he tucked the blade back into a pouch on his utility belt and knelt in front of me. He started to try and lick my pussy through my underwear, but I burst out laughing when I put my hand on his head and I hit a rubbery bat ear instead. He looked up at me and grinned. "Better take it off then, yes?" I agreed and helped him remove the rubbery cowl.

His hair was matted and sweaty from being under the cowl all day, but I didn't care as I put my hands on top of his head and pushed him back to his former position. He started licking me through my panties, soaking them, but I quickly grew frustrated with the unnecessary barrier.

"Take them off," I whined.

"Patience. So greedy."

I started to squirm, I just couldn't help moving my hips, trying to get at his tongue. I could hear him chuckling against my skin as he gripped my hips tight and pinned me hard against the wall. Then I felt his teeth.

Slowly, agonizingly slowly, he drew my panties off my hips. Once past my ass and the tops of my thighs, they fell to the floor.

"Now, where was I? Oh, yeah, I was here," he said before he slid his tongue along my lips and then slipped between them, touching my clit with the tip.

"Jesus, fuck!"

I felt his laugh in my pussy as he flattened his tongue and began to lick, suck, and even bite my clit in all the ways he knew I loved. I was a rocket, ready to explode, and I knew that, at this rate, it wouldn't take me but a moment to orgasm.

"I'm going to come," I moaned, trying to not shout and bring the curious to check out the noises by the ice machine. All I got from him was a thumbs up motion. So I let it happen. I let the most perfect, soul-wrenching orgasm that I had ever had wash over me in undulating waves of pure sensation. It felt like the fucking Fourth of July. Star-spangled awesome.

However, we weren't done. No way was I leaving this alcove without Craig getting his. I pulled him up and tugged at his costume until it lay scattered all over the floor, the spandex suit trapping his ankles, his breathing a bit hoarse, and his magnificent cock at full attention, ready to render service, or be serviced—or both.

"Fuck me."

He moaned at my words, picked me up, and slid right into my wetness. It had been so long I had almost forgotten how big he was and how good it felt to have him deep inside me. With my back pressed against the wall, I wrapped my legs around his waist as he thrust against me, driving himself deeper with each stroke. I felt that sweet tension begin to build again and knew it wouldn't be long until I had another screaming orgasm.

At that moment, a couple cosplayers came into the alcove. I

locked eyes with one of the women as she grabbed her ice. She gave me a smile and a thumbs up on the way out. Like a pro, Craig never broke his stroke, just kept on building up to what I was certain would be our best climax ever.

"I can't wait," he said, his voice a bit hoarse and raspy.

"Then come for me."

He thrust a few more times, hard, and then shuddered, his moans growing louder as he reached the edge.

"That's it, love. Fuck me hard."

My dirty talk sent him over the edge, and he came, buried deep inside me, his body pressed tight against mine. As he continued to grind and shudder through what was an absolutely magnificent climax, I came again, almost as hard as the first time.

As his grip loosened, I slid down his body. Soaking wet, and naked, we gathered our bits and pieces of costuming and snuck back to our room, giggling like teenagers the whole way.

We spent the rest of the evening having sex in the shower, on the counters, and on the floor.

"Didn't you get the memo?" I asked later when we were naked in bed. "Only prop weapons were allowed at the con." He smiled and reached for the weapon on the nightstand, running it gently over my breasts. "This? I won't tell if you won't."

"My lips are sealed," I replied, feeling the cool metal slide over my skin.

"Now *that* would be a shame."

Craig then showed me exactly what he meant.

Mission success.

SMALL CHANGE

D. Fostalove

Keenan placed his order and pulled up to the drive-through window, trying not to smile.

"Happy to have ya! That'll be $9.58," Rashad said before he did a double take at the driver. "Babe, what are you doing here and whose car are you in?"

Keenan handed over the money, exact change. "I'm hungry and it's ours."

Rashad stared blankly at Keenan, too tired to play games with him. "For real, whose car is that?"

"Ours," Keenan said more seriously. "When's your shift over?"

Turning at his shift manager barking for him to hurry up, Rashad tossed the money into the register and asked if Keenan needed condiments or napkins.

"No, we got plenty packs in the fridge." Keenan asked him again when he got off.

Rashad looked at the clock on the wall near him. "About twenty minutes."

"I'll be waiting for you in the parking lot."

Rashad handed him the bag with his food and two medium sodas. "Thanks for choosing Happy Burger. Enjoy."

A knock on the passenger side window brought Keenan from his slumber. He leaned over and unlocked the door to let Rashad inside. Immediately apologizing for the delay, Rashad explained that his manager needed him to stay longer. One of the third-shift workers was running late. Keenan looked at the clock on the dash and realized he'd been waiting for over an hour.

"No prob. You see what I was doing."

Rashad tossed the watered down extra soda out the still open door and replaced it with a fresh one. "Where'd you get this car?"

"You have so many questions." Keenan put the key in the ignition, starting the car. It angrily roared to life. "Just know you don't have to catch two buses to work anymore."

"It's covered in rust . . . "

"Sure is," Keenan said. "It's loud too with no radio. The back windows don't roll down but that's okay because it's ours."

Rashad let out a deep sigh. "I don't want to be a downer . . . "

"Before you start, I got something to share with you."

Interrupting, Rashad asked, "Is this the surprise you were texting about earlier?"

Keenan shook his head.

"There's something else?"

Keenan nodded.

"Okay. I'm all ears."

When they stopped at the traffic light, Keenan retrieved his phone from the console, punched in his voicemail password, and turned on the speakerphone function so Rashad could hear. He watched Rashad's face switch from confusion to pure excitement in a manner of seconds.

"Oh, my God. You got a job! That's great."

"It's a temp-to-perm opportunity working nights but I'm going to make the best of it."

"I'm so happy for you." Rashad leaned over and kissed Keenan on the cheek.

A car honked repeatedly behind them. Keenan looked up to see the light had turned green. Moving his foot from the brake to the gas pedal, the car lurched forward, jerking them violently. Rashad covered his face as the car behind them sped by. Unfazed, Keenan beamed as they moved along the street. Thirty minutes later, the pair arrived at the extended-stay motel where they'd been residing.

Keenan bopped out the car with the food bag while Rashad wearily climbed out the passenger side and walked up the flight of stairs to their second-floor room. Keenan pushed the door aside, allowing Rashad to enter first. He stopped as soon as he stepped inside and turned toward Keenan.

"What is all of this?"

He took another look into the small room that was filled with candles, streamers, and balloons scattered around the floor.

"It's been a good day. I wanted to celebrate."

They stepped into the room, knocking balloons out of their path as they entered. Rashad pulled six dollars' worth of quarters from both of his pockets and neatly stacked them on the table next to an older model thirty-two-inch television.

"I already did the laundry," Keenan said.

"Then we'll save them for next time." Rashad continued surveying the room. "I can't believe you really cleaned up."

Keenan smiled and grabbed Rashad's hand, pulling him toward the bed.

"I'm tired and my feet hurt. I want to soak in some Epsom salts."

Laughing, Keenan said, "You sound like an old man."

"I feel like one, been standing for almost ten hours."

A change in Rashad's disposition made Keenan ask him what was wrong.

"Tell me you didn't spend a lot of money on this stuff."

"Everything came from the dollar store," Keenan said. "I have the receipt if you wanna see."

Rashad counted aloud. "The fast food was ten . . . how much was this?"

Keenan pulled the receipt from his wallet and held it up.

"Ten seventy." Rashad inspected the receipt in greater detail. "Why did you buy soda? I get it free from work."

"I wanted grape. Y'all don't have that."

Rashad sighed.

"Don't be upset."

Continuing to read each line item on the receipt, Rashad grumbled. "Cleaning supplies?"

Keenan pulled the slip from Rashad's grip. "That's enough."

"We don't need flowery-smelling antibacterial 'whatever'."

"I'm tired of 'borrowing' bleach and other stuff from the housekeeping supply closet."

Rashad turned to Keenan, who was using a pack of hotel matches to light the candles strategically placed around the room.

"Did you pay up the room for next week?"

Keenan nodded. "Now stop worrying and come over here. Let me take care of you."

Rashad reluctantly sat on the bed next to Keenan, who leaned over and kissed him.

"Things are starting to look up for us."

"We've been here before," Rashad reminded him. "Things were going okay and then in a flash, they were bad again, real bad."

Keenan grabbed his hand and put it in his lap. "It'll be different this time. I can feel it."

"When are you going to tell me where you got the money to pay for that car outside?" Rashad asked after a moment of silence. "You know I'm going to keep asking."

"Selling plasma and my Jordan 11s."

"Wait. What?"

"Yeah . . . I know."

"Why did you do that?"

"For us."

Keenan explained how having the automobile would drastically cut Rashad's commute to work. He added he would also need transportation for his overnight gig since buses stopped running at midnight.

"Which pair are those exactly?"

"The *Space Jam* ones."

Rashad squeezed his hand and thanked him for the big gesture. Keenan's small collection of Jordans meant everything to him and the fact he'd sold a pair for them spoke volumes to exactly where their relationship ranked in his life.

"If everything goes good with this job, we can be out of this dump by the end of the year."

"I hope you're right."

Keenan pulled Rashad's cap off and undid the buttons of his work shirt before kissing him on the neck. Rashad playfully shrugged him off.

"Don't you start with me," he said. "I told you I was tired."

"Good. Then you won't have much fight in you."

"Uh huh."

Returning to Rashad's neck, Keenan said, "I love when you come home smelling like fries."

"If you're hungry, I have something you can eat."

Keenan sat back so he could see Rashad's face. "Is that right?"

"Let me stop being a tease."

"No. Keep on. I like it."

Rashad adjusted on the bed, sighing deeply before leaning forward with both hands over his face. Keenan grabbed the soda from the nightstand, taking a sip. He offered Rashad some but he declined as he sat back up, stress etched in his face.

"Wanna talk about your day?"

"Not really."

They became quiet, the noise from the colorful array of tenants seeping into their room.

"I can't believe I finally got a *real* job."

"I know. I'm so excited for you."

"Guess how much they offered."

Rashad threw out two different figures, Keenan shaking his head both times. "Just tell me."

"Fifteen fifty an hour!"

Rashad perked up. "Are you serious?"

Keenan nodded. "Crazy, right?"

"That's almost twice what I make at the booger palace."

Chuckling, Keenan said he knew. That was the main reason he accepted the job, the pay. It would completely turn their lives around.

"So let's celebrate."

"And how do you want to do that?"

Keenan moved Rashad's hand over the crotch area of his jeans.

"You know exactly how."

"Let me take a shower and gather myself."

"Want me to heat up the leftover burger for when you get out?"

Standing, Rashad shook his head. "Quisha got me a salad when she went out on her break."

"I'll be here when you get out."

When he stepped out of the bathroom, wearing only a towel, Rashad was inundated by the coconut scent from the candles. Keenan was sprawled across the bed. A bundle of fabric and a bottle of lotion were on the bed beside him. Rashad eyed the items before taking in Keenan.

"Where did you get those?" Rashad had noticed the lace boxer briefs.

"Picked 'em up earlier." Keenan shifted in the bed, modeling them. "I know you like when I wrap *it* up real nice for you."

"You're spending the money before we even get it."

"It was on clearance for $9.99. It's not the end of the world."

"I thought we talked about this before."

"Come here."

Rashad approached slowly, still somewhat peeved.

"We are going to be all right. I promise. Okay?"

Rashad nodded.

"Now get in the bed with me."

When Rashad climbed into the bed, Keenan hopped up with the bottle of lotion.

"Where are you going?"

Keenan squeezed lotion into his palms.

"You look so good right now."

"Thank you."

The shower had energized Rashad. He'd trimmed his goatee and oiled up before reentering the room, knowing Keenan preferred him clean shaven. Watching him at the foot of the bed, Rashad admired the green fabric against Keenan's dark skin. He had a stunning physique with a boyish face even though he was closer to thirty than twenty.

Their eyes met, Keenan still rubbing the liquid in his hands. "Like what you see?"

"Yes, indeed." Rashad caught a whiff of the lotion. "What is that?"

"Soothing spearmint with eucalyptus."

"Smells nice."

Keenan knelt at the end of the bed and grabbed one of Rashad's feet, massaging it. Rashad closed his eyes, melting into the pillows. Keenan spent what felt like forever on one foot, caressing each inch, before moving to the other, spending just as much time on it as the first.

"You don't know how good that feels."

"Glad you like."

After finishing with Rashad's feet, Keenan began massaging his calves. Inching upward, he moved the towel aside to work on Rashad's thighs before kissing his flaccid member. Rashad opened his eyes at that moment, peering down as Keenan glanced up at him with a seductive smile on his face.

"I'm going to take care of you tonight."

He planted a series of quick kisses on Rashad's inner thighs.

"No."

Keenan stopped, confused. "What?"

"You sold a pair of shoes from your collection, donated plasma, cleaned up the room and decorated it, all for us," Rashad said. "Let me show my appreciation."

Rashad patted the space on the bed next to him. Keenan moved from between Rashad's legs and rested on his back on the open spot.

"You took these from the drawer to use, right?"

"Yeah." Keenan grabbed one of the neckties and dangled it over Rashad's body. "We haven't played in a long time. Tonight feels like a good time."

Maneuvering to the side of the small bed, Rashad instructed Keenan to move to the center where he'd arranged their pillows. "Prop yourself up on those."

Keenan scooted to the middle and raised his arms instinctively. Rashad tied one to each bedpost.

"What's the third one for?"

"Blindfold me. Gag me. Doesn't matter."

Rashad considered his options, choosing to restrict Keenan's sight. He wanted to hear his moans, exchange dirty banter during their session. With the third necktie wrapped tightly around Keenan's eyes, Rashad climbed out of the bed and watched him twist about, testing the arm restraints.

"Tight enough for you?"

"You always are."

"I'm not talking about me."

"But I am."

Rashad could see the lace underwear tighten around Keenan's erection.

"What do you want me to do?"

"Whatever you want."

"You sure?"

Keenan nodded. "I love when you control me."

Rashad scanned the room, finding the feather duster in one of the chairs at a small dining table. It was another of the items they'd "borrowed" from the hotel's supply closet. He grabbed it and returned to Keenan, waiting in anticipation.

"You got me nervous."

Rashad chuckled. "You should be."

When the feathers grazed his feet, Keenan jerked them away. Rashad quickly moved around the bed to where Keenan had moved them.

"You are so mean," Keenan managed between laughter as

Rashad moved from his feet to his stomach and exposed under-arms.

Rashad loved hearing Keenan's hysterical giggling. It was infectious. They laughed loudly, Keenan squirming all over the bed to avoid the unseen object. His attempts were futile though. Rashad quickly found his desired targets wherever Keenan managed to move to.

"Please stop," Keenan pleaded while wheezing from laughter.

"Nope." Rashad continued his assault on Keenan's ticklish regions. "I can do this all night."

"I'm going to piss myself or pass out."

Easing up, Rashad moved the duster along his arms lightly, causing him to fidget. He leaned down and kissed Keenan before setting the cleaning tool onto the nightstand.

"I've tortured you enough." Rashad straddled Keenan in the bed.

He could feel Keenan instantly relax beneath him.

"Thank you. Don't know how much more I could take."

"I'm not done with you yet."

"I know."

Rashad reached for a candle on the nightstand and brought it close to Keenan's skin.

"Do it."

"Do what?"

"Like last time."

"You sure?"

"Yeah."

Rashad tilted the candle slightly. The hot liquid moved to the edge before freefalling, landing on Keenan's stomach. He flinched, his muscles flexing.

"Wow."

"Too much?"

Keenan shook his head.

"Say it."

"Pour it on me."

Rashad carefully angled the candle again.

"Ooh," Keenan moaned, surprised as the wax connected with one of his nipples. "More."

As Keenan gritted his teeth, Rashad could feel his erection throbbing between them.

"You okay?"

"Yeah. Keep going."

Rashad continued to slowly drip the hot wax onto Keenan's body, each droplet's connection causing him to tense up in pain and pleasure. Rashad set the candle on the nightstand when all the available liquid had been dripped over Keenan. He picked up a takeout menu and began fanning it over Keenan until the liquid had solidified.

Using a fingernail, Rashad peeled wax off one of Keenan's nipples. He leaned down and kissed the spot where the wax had been. He continued picking at various spots on Keenan's body where wax had landed, kissing each spot after he'd scratched most of it off.

"We'll remove the rest later." Rashad climbed off of Keenan and yanked lightly at his lace underwear. "Get out of these."

Keenan lifted his butt enough for Rashad to remove the boxer briefs for him. He slid Keenan out of the underwear and tossed them onto the floor before he climbed up onto Keenan again. He pressed their erect dicks against each other in his fist and began to slowly stroke both.

"You like that?"

Keenan nodded. "Feels incredible."

Rashad gyrated his hips as he gripped their erections.

"Want me to slob on it before I slide it inside and ride it?"

"Yeah, do that."

"What if I tossed your legs back and started drilling you until you couldn't take it anymore?"

"Don't tease me."

He kept stroking while continuing to throw out different scenarios.

"I like when you're nasty."

"Do you?"

Keenan nodded.

Rashad spit on him. "Nasty like that?"

"Yeah, just like that."

With an open palm, Rashad smeared the saliva in Keenan's face before kissing him. He then returned to stroking them.

"Choke me."

"What?"

Keenan repeated himself. "You got me so close. Choke me."

"Is that what you want?"

He nodded.

"Say it."

"Choke me. You know, the way I like it."

"Knock on the headboard if you want me to stop."

"Like usual."

"But you never want me to . . . "

Using the hand he'd been stroking himself with, Rashad clamped his fingers around Keenan's throat and squeezed. Keenan tensed up at first but relaxed as Rashad continued to jack him off.

"Tight enough for you?"

Keenan attempted to speak but his words came out garbled. Rashad kept stroking him, faster than before. His fingernails dug into Keenan's throat. Suddenly Keenan jerked wildly under him as he began releasing glob after glob into the air. His excitement landed everywhere, including Rashad's face and chest. As Keenan relaxed beneath him, Rashad released both holds he had. Keenan let out a deep exhale, both hands falling limp in their restraints.

"You okay?"

"Yeah," he panted. "I think I almost blacked out."

The thought frightened Rashad but he knew that's what Keenan wanted, to reach the edge of consciousness. Those orgasms were the ultimate to him. He removed the blindfold, followed by the neckties binding Keenan's hands and rested on the bed beside him.

"What about you?" Keenan asked.

"What about me?"

"You didn't bust one."

Rashad patted him on the thigh. "I can wait for round two."

"Another round, huh?"

"Yes."

"What makes you think there will be a second?"

"I'm not finished with you just yet."

SINKING IN
THE SUMMER

Leah Sage

The Little Piney was always cold. That was a good thing.
Rivers fed by cold springs never had any snakes. At least, not
in the water. It was the branches that hung overhead that you
had to be wary of. She loved that river. Had from the first time
she had set a kayak in it and started paddling. That first trip with
a small group of friends had been a twelve-hour-long adventure.
They'd had no idea just how far away the launch point really
was. Or how far past the campsite the second pick-up would be.
It was a trial by ordeal and they learned quickly how to read the
water, feel a capsize coming, flip themselves back over, and bail
without losing their paddles or kayaks to the river.

It should, by all rights, have been a horrible experience. By
the end of it, they were bone weary, bruised, half-drowned,
and freezing. Anna had never in her life enjoyed a challenge
quite that much. She came back the next year, and the one after
that, and after that, and eventually even took on the two-day,
twenty-hour route, camping around the ten-hour mark when

they found a spot they liked. That one was difficult, but that summer had been dry and the water had been low. They'd spent more time hauling gear down river than in a kayak.

That wasn't true for her second attempt. There had been plenty of rain that spring and through the early summer and the water was high and moving quickly. There would be only a few places along the way that they'd need to hop out and drag the kayaks over hundreds of tiny, slippery rocks worn round by the currents. Every smooth, deep swimming hole would be filled well past its usual bank. Of course, the wise knew not too swim too deeply. The Little Piney was beautiful, and small as rivers went, but it boasted an undercurrent that could suck down even seasoned swimmers.

The springs, too, would be higher than usual. Fast water always flooded from the little tributaries that fed the Piney. Usually only about ankle deep, but moving with a force that had shocked her the first time she'd discovered it. If one cared to stop—as she had to enjoy the scents of Spanish moss and crisp, cold water—there were always interesting things to discover. Her favorite was a path that led back into the woods. At a fork, the left wound higher and away from the spring to what remained of a French fur-trapper's cabin built well before Missouri had been a US territory. The right led them down past white rapids to the very heart of the spring. There it was crystal clear, calm, still waters. The only disturbance little air bubbles rising to the surface.

Not many swam there, but there were carefully placed stones that led from the path down to the spring itself, which was almost entirely walled off by dark-black stone on the north, east, and west sides. To the south, the rapids could distantly be heard, but no longer seen. Along the eastern curve of dark stone, at the bottom of the rudimentary, natural staircase, was sand so white it almost looked like bleached sugar. When the water was low, it was mostly solid. A normal beach you could throw a towel down on and relax so long as you avoided the water's edge. When the water was high, if you looked closely, you could see those little air bubbles escaping from time to time, the springs boiling away just beneath the surface.

She'd never thought to risk it before. This time, however, it was exactly why she was there.

And why she had invited Alex to come with her.

Anna was crouched down on the last stone above the small beach. Her left hand was braced against the rock wall, and her right slowly moved back and forth over the soft sand. She could feel the cold beneath it. It sent a little chill up her arm, but she was no stranger to swimming around in cold springs. What could be deeply stressful for some was bracing and soothing to her. The way walking barefoot in the snow could center a chaotic mind and bring focus and clarity in the middle of an emotional storm.

Above her, halfway down the rocky staircase and waiting with a patient restraint that never ceased to astound her, Alex stood, quietly watching her. Anna imagined she could feel his anticipation. She knew he was just as thrilled to be there as she was, but it still radiated off him in a way that raised goose flesh on her arms where the impending cold hadn't. She knew without looking that he was watching her closely. The weight of his attention was as real and tangible a thing as the smooth rock beneath her feet. There was no rush, though. No pressure to get on with it. She was going to sink for him, and Alex seemed more than content to allow her to take her time.

When Anna straightened and looked up to where he stood, she found him waiting with a wide smile that twisted slowly into a wicked grin. A small backpack rested over his shoulder, within it was a rope and a few other things, just in case. Alex managed to look comfortable and relaxed in a T-shirt and swim trunks when she felt anything but at ease. He raised an eyebrow at her, a warm breeze upsetting his dark hair, and then one arm moved in an "after you" gesture. Anna smirked up at him, but her heart beat hard against her ribs as her anticipation built.

Pulling off her river shoes and the light swimsuit cover that protected her pale skin from the sun, Anna held them out and gave them a wiggle to lure him closer. "I won't try to pull you in, I swear," she told him, earning a low, dry laugh.

"Not afraid I might push you in?" Alex teased her back, but obligingly came down the last few steps to take her things.

With him so close it was difficult to resist her desire to kiss him. She always seemed to be wanting to kiss him. Anna smirked at herself, shaking her head, and blushed a soft pink at the curious look he gave her. Instead of answering, she turned to face the cool beach, and then hesitated a moment to decide if she should take off her dark blue bikini or risk losing it in the sand.

Warm, strong fingers closed over her own. There was a quiet kind of reassurance and comfort in Alex's touch, as well as a question. He was over the moon that she'd surprise him with his own, secret fantasy, but he didn't want Anna doing anything she didn't want to do, either. When she nodded that she was okay, Alex gave her hand a gentle squeeze. "Go ahead. I've got you."

Anna peeked over her shoulder to smile at him and squeezed his hand to silently say *thank you* before taking that first step out into the sand. She held her breath, heartbeat thundering in her ears. A soft squeak left her throat when she sank a little further than she was ready for. Not far, really. The sand barely covered up to her mid-calf, but she hadn't really thought it'd go past her ankle.

"You, okay?" There was dry amusement in Alex's voice that

had Anna shooting him a dry look despite her face turning a
vivid red. His smile only grew, and after squeezing her fingers
once more, he let go of her hand and stepped back to watch her
progress.

Quicksand isn't quite the same as mud in a number of ways,
but what she noticed first was that as she took a few careful
steps further out, she didn't seem to need to fight the suction of
a vacuum forming around her. The sand shifted relatively easily,
more like very thick water. It didn't quite grip at her body and
hold on, but rather caressed, massaged, and sometimes tickled.
The weight of it pressed in around her, the coolness not as bad
as she first imagined it would be. She felt childish, playing in the
sand and wiggling her legs to watch the surface jiggle like jelly.
At the same time, a tense excitement and instinctive fear were
making her breathing quick and shallow.

A bit sooner than Anna would have liked, she was up to her
knees in the sand, and could feel herself slowly, so slowly, sinking deeper without even moving. Alex watched from the edge
where he had moved back up the stone steps for a better view of
her. His tongue passed over his lips, feeling his own excitement
already building. His movement caught her attention and Anna
glanced up, momentarily pausing in her effort to walk out closer
to where the pale sand met the water's edge.

He smiled. She blushed worse. His smile grew.

Another step further and he heard one of those little whines
she made when some way he touched or kissed her felt particularly good. A collection of emotions and expressions crossed
her face too quickly for him to catch them all. The sand was
crawling up her thighs and he caught that flutter in them when
she shivered. Alex couldn't have looked away if he'd tried. His
eyes darted from the color that curled down her neck and across
her chest, to the bounce and jiggle of her breasts and ass as she

shifted and struggled within the sand's grip. That steady progress down was a delightful tease to him, as was every sound Anna made as she slowly sank deeper.

"How are you doing?" Alex called out to her.

"All right, I think," Anna's voice was nervous and shaky. So were her hands as she ran them down over her belly, but she chuckled, and then let out a slow breath. As the sand crept up her legs, a whimpered moan left her lips. Anticipation, she thought, of a sensation that was beginning to become just as familiar as a lover's touch. It had started the first time she had gone sinking for him, in the silt around a pond behind a cabin in the desert. That one had been a happy accident.

What had looked like solid earth—the cracked and dried bottom of an old pond—had turned out to be thick, deep mud. As soon as it had grabbed her, she'd been trapped, unable to escape the vacuum that formed as she sank deeper. If Alex hadn't been in earshot that day, Anna still believed she wouldn't have made it. He'd gotten her out, cleaned her up, and made sure she was okay before he admitted that he wished he'd gotten to see it.

Each time since, and again there in the quicksand, that creeping touch that squeezed in around her thighs felt too much like hands sliding up her legs. It was like waiting for the brush of a tongue or fingers to swipe across her nether lips for the first time. The higher the sand crept the worse her body shivered and the louder she moaned.

Alex didn't miss a single breath of those sounds, keenly aware of the effect the sand was having on Anna. Her softening and tensing expressions and body language would have told him everything he needed to know regardless, but he enjoyed the noises she made. A few smart-ass comments came to him, but Alex let them go unspoken. He didn't want to break the spell she was under and miss a second of her descent into pleasure.

Anna took a deep breath in, her breasts rising against the confines of the meager bikini top, and he watched as her throat worked on a slow swallow. Pale gray eyes flicked in his direction, and then darted away again. The color in her skin flushed and Alex watched her curiously, wondering what she was thinking. His questions were answered before he could ask them, and his breathing quickened as Anna reached shaking hands behind her back to tug at the little bow that held her top in place. The laces came undone easily and she tossed the scraps of blue fabric toward the bottom of the stone steps. Alex's tongue passed over his lips again in a subconscious display of desire as his fingers twitched. The pack on his shoulder hit the ground by his feet, but he didn't move. It was getting more difficult to keep himself in place, but he managed it by reminding himself that there was still more to see.

Anna squirmed in the sand, twisting her legs and rocking her hips to help work herself deeper into its cool and tightening grip. The cold was getting worse and she thought she felt water up to her knees, but she wasn't entirely sure about where the sand ended and the water began . . . if there was even a dividing line to feel. Her mind was focused elsewhere, anyway. She was mesmerized by just how different the soft sand was from the smooth silt and how it had stroked and sucked at her body.

The sand didn't cling to her skin, or pull at it as she moved. Instead, as she worked her hips down into its cool, patient grip, it obligingly rubbed, massaged, and pushed against her. Slowly, the sand parted the damp outer lips of her pussy by pushing up against her bikini bottoms. The soft fabric bunched up between her lips and was pulled tight. She could feel the sand pushing against it as she rocked her hips, so many tiny points of sensation grinding across that thin barrier. A soft whine escaped her, and then a low, eager moan. Anna's head tipped back and her

body shook, hips rolling to grind eagerly against that new sensation to get more of it. Back and forth, wherever she moved,
the cool sand pressed into her, shifted for her, obligingly moved
across her skin like dozens of caressing fingers, and patiently let
her wiggle her way deeper.

Closer to the water's edge, it was a little bit easier to move. Or
maybe it was just that adrenaline and pleasure had helped her to
forget that she was supposed to be afraid. The sand climbed up
her stomach, the surface shifting with the obvious movements
of her body. Alex didn't have to guess what was going on and
didn't bother hiding his interest or arousal when she looked his
way again. She was brightly flushed, biting at that full lower lip,
and looking very pleased with herself. He had shed his T-shirt to
be forgotten somewhere on the ground and his cock was making an impressive tent out of his shorts. Anna smiled at him. He
smiled back, admiring the way her breasts were lifted up as she
continued to sink, almost as if sand was helping to put her on
display for him.

The honey-colored skin around her nipples seemed darker
against the bright sand, the soft pink nipples that tipped them
tight and swollen and turning a darker red as he watched. Anna
made a stunning picture, head tipped back and her hands cupping each breast to squeeze them. Alex's own heartbeat thun-
dered in his ears while he enjoyed the view. Their eyes met for
another fleeting moment, but he could see that his attention and
the sand that was slowly claiming her were turning Anna on
even more. While most of her body was hidden from him, he
could tell she was still moving. Those unmistakable sounds of
pleasure started anew, and again; he kept all his responses to
himself, mesmerized by her darkening blush and eager delight.

Anna was almost neck deep when she stopped sinking,
whether from reaching a point of buoyancy or reaching the

bottom, she didn't really know—or bother to care. Her attention had narrowed down to the desperate need for relief. One hand worked its way down under the sand, fingers following the contours of her body to find her clit. She teased that tender bundle of nerves through the soft fabric that had bunched up over it. Pleasure flared up so hot and fast it startled her. It spread quickly, tearing a shout loose from her throat. All around her the sand pressed in tightly. It was almost as if a lazy, indulgent lover had turned greedy and demanding at the first sign of the orgasm that was fast approaching. She was trapped, the sand had her, and it wasn't going to let her go. Dozens of unseen hands held her tightly, stroking and caressing every inch of her body. Her hips rocked and the sand drank her arousal as it leaked from her. Squirming, wriggling, Anna couldn't escape its grasp, couldn't pull herself loose, and every movement sent a thousand points of sensation running across her skin.

All Alex could do was watch. He knew the hints, those little signs in how her body shook and the sounds she made. He wanted her desperately, a thing that grew worse as he watched Anna strain, getting closer, then closer still. Her eyes opened; their gazes locked. He had no idea what she was thinking, feeling, but he knew exactly what was happening to her body. Sounds he knew well, cries that were music to his ears came out of her. Across her face he could see the spell that the sand, lust, and her imagination had wrought. That climax was wonderful to watch, and to hear. So was the desperately slow recovery that kept Anna whimpering far longer than usual.

"Help, please," she eventually rasped out, and Alex grinned. It didn't sound at all like she had gotten over that orgasm yet.

Gathering up the backpack, he took out a spike, a mallet, and the bundle of rope. Alex walked back down the stone steps, found a good place to hammer that spike into the rock wall, and then tied one end of the rope around it. Looking out to where Anna waited and watched him, he pulled off his swim trunks to toss them aside. Her eyes darted down to the proof of his enjoyment, and he grinned at the way she blushed, not the least bit inclined to hide just how hard his cock was for her.

Rope firmly in hand, Alex started to make his way out to Anna. She really hadn't gotten all that far. He got within a foot or so of her, standing over her, not having sank near as much— he wasn't rocking himself among other things—and grinned wickedly down at the expectant look she gave him.

She reached one arm up to him and Alex growled two phrases at her. The first made Anna smirk at him; the second twisted her lips into a wicked little grin that mirrored his own.

"Good girl," he told her. "Now convince me."

Her answer, though her voice shook with desire, was crystal clear. "Come closer."

Alex wrapped his fingers gently but firmly around Anna's wrist and pulled, raising her up from the sand and sinking himself a little deeper. His other hand kept a secure grip on the rope as he watched her lips part and her tongue flatten into a soft bed. He let his head fall back as the wet heat of her mouth closed around him, restraining that instinctive need to rock his hips while her talented lips and tongue worked on him. He groaned his pleasure and Anna moaned her delight, each feeding off the other's pleasure to drive each other to new heights.

Alex hadn't meant to let her finish him. He'd had so many plans of the things he wanted to do to Anna, the orgasms he wanted to give her to repay her for indulging his fetish and enjoying it with him. Her lips pulled, her tongue stroked, and then she took him down into the tight, grasping channel of her throat. His hips rocked with a will of their own and Alex roared his release. His body burned and shook while Anna drank him

down. Best of all was that desire-drunk and very feminine satisfaction she glowed with while she licked him clean.

Alex felt utterly weak when she was done with him, but he
still had to rescue them both from the quicksand. With what
little focus and will he had left, he tied a loop around Anna's
wrist to be sure they didn't lose the rope, and then he tucked his
arms beneath her own and sat back onto the sand. The feel of
her weight and warmth against him made him smile, particularly when she nuzzled against his chest to breathe in his scent.

Arm over arm, he dragged them back and out of the sand,
Anna helping by wiggling her legs to keep them from being
caught. When they finally reached the safe section of beach,
they both collapsed. Grinning and panting and gasping, the pair
clung weakly to each other until their hearts slowed and the
world settled back into place around them.

"That was . . . really good," Alex said as soon as he trusted
his voice to work, enjoying the afterglow and the feeling of her
smooth body curled around his.

"Fantastic," Anna murmured back. "I'm so glad you told me."

"I'm glad you didn't think I was crazy," he admitted with
a rueful smile. There were still a couple of hours of paddling
to do before they would reach the first good campsite, but she
didn't seem ready to move, and he wasn't exactly interested in
anything that meant he had to let go of her.

"You're not crazy," Anna chuckled, a dark, warm sound
Alex had come to recognize meant his woman was thinking
about something he was going to enjoy. Thoroughly. He tightened his arms around her and she purred a warm, contented
sound.

"You're very good to me," he told her.

"It's only fair," Anna said through a yawn, making him grin
again. "You are good to me."

"Might as well get rid of the bottoms, too," Alex suggested, his voice still thick and rough in a way that made Anna smirk up at him. It took little effort to squirm her way free of the wet, sand-covered fabric, but Anna still collapsed tiredly against him when she was done. There was a special kind of temptation in that little triangle of bare skin that was pristine, while the rest of her body held traces of wet sand almost everywhere. His fingers twitched, but Alex let that desire go unexplored.

Instead, they rested there together, dozing in the heat of late afternoon under the speckled shadows cast by the high forest canopy. They listened to the distant sounds of the rapids, the various bird songs that echoed around them, and each other's breathing. They'd have to get up and move on eventually, but that place had become something special. Something sacred.

Anna loved the Little Piney. It always ran cold. And after that visit, Alex would look forward to their kayaking trips, and taking time off to go sinking in the summer.

THE PINK LADY

Birch Rosen

'm lying casually on my stomach in bed when Cassidy finishes her voice feminization practice and comes into the bedroom. Her hair is bright pink, freshly dyed a few days ago.

My pose is a ruse. Up until a few seconds ago, I'd been kneeling on the bed, fucking my hand with my soaking wet cunt. When I heard Cassidy's footsteps, though, I pulled up the soft lounge pants I've been wearing all day and assumed my nonchalant position.

"I have a surprise for you," I tell her.

"Is it . . . you finished your book?" she asks.

"No."

"Is it . . . the cat's under the blanket?" she tries with a smile.

"No. Pull down my pants," I say. I get on my hands and knees, ass right at the side of the bed to give her easy access.

I'm not sure what it is with me lately. I haven't been this horny since I first started testosterone, and it's been almost four years now. Granted, I was watching porn while Cassidy did her voice practice, but that doesn't fully explain how wet I am either. I haven't made quite as much natural lubrication since I started T, but right now I'm soaking. It's thin and slick, spilling out of my cunt, enough that it coated my fingers earlier without making the inside or outside feel any less wet.

Cassidy pulls down my pants and rubs a couple of fingers up and down my wet hole. There's no resistance. She rubs my dick between her fingers, and the arch of my back deepens.

"That's a nice surprise," she says. "Wait while I grab some things." She retrieves my paddle and sets it on the bedding I've pushed out of the way. *Oh*. She steps into the closet and comes back with a blindfold. She's blindfolded me before, but not for a while. Most of our sex these days is more vanilla—not for lack of interest in kink, but just because we've settled into a routine over the last several years. But I can tell this is about to be elaborate.

"Put this on," she says, handing me the blindfold. I close my eyes, covering them before lying back down with my ass in the air. The fit of the blindfold is comfortable, and I could check to make sure I can't see at all, but I know I'll keep my eyes closed on principle regardless.

Cassidy starts spanking me with the paddle, randomly alternating sides of my body, areas of my ass and upper thighs, and strengths of strikes. Sometimes she rubs the surface of the paddle in little circles on my skin to soothe or tease me. Speaking of teasing, she sinks down to breathe warm air onto my cunt and dick without making contact. After some more spanking, she finally takes my cock into her mouth, and I rock back against her face. I know she likes it when I do.

Then, standing again, she rubs my back hole.

"Are you ready to have this filled?" she asks.

"Yes," I say. An understatement.

Cassidy presses a lubed-up steel plug against my hole and slowly works it in. The coldness of the plug makes it feel bigger somehow, and I briefly wonder if she's actually using a steel *dildo*, but then I feel the plug taper back down.

"Is that all you're gonna fill me up with?" I ask.

"You'll just have to wait and see," she says. I hear her washing her hands in the other room, then feel her climbing onto the bed from the side, positioning herself in front of me and straightening up on her knees.

"It's time for you to suck this hard cock," she says.

I take her thick girldick into my mouth, feeling her skin on my tongue. It's hot and smooth. She's as hard as I've ever felt her, and throbbing. I bob my head a few times, lubing up her shaft with my mouth, then take her as deep as I can. I feel her in my throat. I can't breathe when she's this deep inside me, so I don't hold it for long. I gag a little on some of my deeper strokes, but I feel in control, and the thick saliva that fills my mouth makes it easier as I go.

"Feel the plug inside you and imagine being spit-roasted," Cassidy tells me. She knows I haven't gotten much time to play with my newer lover yet, let alone make introductions and play with both of them, but *God* I want to. The only question is which of them I'd want in which hole, but for now I don't have to decide.

"That's enough for now," Cassidy says, pulling out of my mouth. I swallow my saliva as she moves across the bed to get behind me again.

"Would you like my cock in another hole?" she asks.

"Yes," I moan, almost adding, "Mistress." We haven't used the honorific before, but I feel like she'd like it.

Her mouth is near my ear now.

"As if you have a choice," she says in a low, condescending

tone. Then she breaks role for a moment to whisper, "You do—
you do have a choice." I don't feel like interrupting what's happening, but I'll have to tell her when we're done that I don't need
the in-the-moment affirmation.

"Which hole?" she asks. She's standing behind me at the side
of the bed now.

"The extra one," I say. It's so wet, and it hasn't had anything
in it since Cassidy came into the room. She slides in easily and
starts thrusting.

"Oh, wow, I can feel the plug," she says. I'm not surprised.
I can feel where the plug and her dick press against each other
through the soft, wet tissue inside me. I thrust back against her
as she fucks me.

"What if you fucked two of my holes at once?" I ask.

"Like with my fingers?"

"Uh-huh."

She pulls out and steps away for a moment. I hear the soft
thump of a towel landing on the bed in front of me. I shudder
and moan as she removes the plug from my ass and places it on
the towel. Then a warm finger takes its place. When she resumes
thrusting, her finger bobs in and out of me in sync with her
thrusts as I'd hoped it would. It's more satisfying than the plug.
I feel like I might be able to come like this, even without direct
stimulation to my dick.

"I can feel my clit through you," Cassidy says. Again, I'm
not surprised. I've fingered myself in both holes simultaneously
before, and I know how thin the wall dividing them is. It must
feel amazing to touch her own clit through me. I feel good, the
crown of my head pleasantly buzzing.

After fucking me that way for a while, Cassidy tells me she
needs her tits sucked. She puts the plug back in my ass and
guides me—still blindfolded—up and into a sitting position

with my back against the headboard. She straddles my lap, and I use my hands first to orient myself to her body, then to pull her close and feel the skin all over her back and sides as I suck her nipples hard. I haven't had erotic feeling in my nipples since top surgery, but I remember how good it used to feel. I like making Cassidy feel good, and I also take pleasure in the texture of her nipples in my mouth, the way she arches and moans as I roll my tongue around them.

Cassidy pulls back and lowers herself to kiss me on the lips. "What does my face smell like?" she asks me. I know she likes how it smells when she's been sucking my dick. She'll tell me periodically throughout the day, until she washes her face at night, "My face smells horny!"

I inhale deeply but don't smell myself on her yet, so I answer, "Hmm . . . like face?"

"I'll have to make the smell a little clearer, then," she says.

She lowers herself to suck my dick again and I slide my hips forward to give her better access.

"Put your hands on the back of my head," she tells me.

Usually it's hard for me to dominate her, even though I know she wants me to, even though I'm familiar with the desire to submit. I'm grateful when a trusted person dominates me, but when it's my turn, I usually struggle even to really pull hair. It's not that I don't want to, just that there's this part of me that's preoccupied with how I'm "supposed" to treat people and slow to acknowledge that well-established consent expands the range of appropriate treatment.

This time, though, I'm in the moment. Maybe it's the blind-fold, or maybe it's easier for me to approach domming from a submissive angle, following instructions about what to do. I obey Cassidy, wrapping both hands around the back of her head, and take it a little further, even, pulling her head closer and using my control to get the exact pressure and positioning I want. I can feel the shape of her skull under her skin. I'd know to pause and check in if she tapped me, made a hesitant noise, or pulled against my hands, but she doesn't. She moans into me and I know she's loving it. I fuck her face, my moans joining hers. She pauses her sucking occasionally to lick me or take a deep breath.

A little breathless, she sits up to kiss me again. Her lips are warm from going down on me, and now she tastes like me.

"How does my face smell now?" she asks.

"Like cock. Mmm, two cocksuckers kissing," I say with a smile.

"What's gayer than that?" she says.

Cassidy offers to fuck my ass now that it's all warmed up, and I accept. She maneuvers the towel under me. I tilt my hips up to help her get the plug out. She sets it down on the towel again, and I hear her lubing up her dick. She slides in easily. My body has been hungry for this. Cassidy gives me lube to rub my own dick with.

As she continues, a bit later, she tells me, "If you like, I'll get you a tool you can use."

"Oh? What kind of tool?" I ask.

Without pulling out of me, she reaches over to my bedside drawer, retrieves my Magic Wand, and places it in my hand.

"You can use this on any part of your body." I feel an exception looming in the odd inclusivity of her permission, but I start to move the vibrator down to my dick. She grabs my hand.

". . . Except that." She releases my hand. I think for a second, then raise the head of the vibrator to what I hope is her tit. She didn't say I *couldn't*. I turn it on, and Cassidy shakes and moans.

"Very creative." She continues fucking me but makes me wait for my vibrator.

"Very well, you can use it on your dick."

I moan, contracting around Cassidy, as the vibrator makes contact. I know the pressure of my ass is too much for her sometimes, but it's an involuntary pleasure response. Her dick pops out, and she tries once to slide it back in before telling me, "I'm gonna use one of my other cocks to make you come."

I can tell by touch which one this is: a recent favorite with dual-density silicone. We call it the Pink Lady because this is a girldick-loving household and, like Cassidy's hair, it's bright pink. She alternates lubing up the tip and pressing it against my hole until it slides in for the first time. I moan deeply and press harder into my vibrator.

"I'm going to have to take this out and put more lube on it, okay?" Cassidy asks. "But it's going to feel even better when it slides back in." I don't respond. It *is* dragging a little bit, and it *will* feel better with more lube, but I'm absorbed in sensations I don't want to lose, even for a few seconds.

"I want you to say, 'Yes, Mistress.' Can you do that for me?" *Ha! I really should've called her "Mistress" earlier!*

"Yes, Mistress," I manage between moans. I whimper as she pulls the dildo out.

"Aww, my poor slut, you must feel so empty without this cock in you."

"Yes, Mistress," I whine.

I gasp in pleasure as the Pink Lady easily slides back into me.

"Now isn't that better?" Cassidy asks.

"Yes, Mistress!"

She slides her hand over my thigh. I'm starting to get close.

"Mistress, may I come?" I ask. It feels vulnerable, almost dangerous, like running my finger along the blade of a knife. I like feeling close to orgasm, but it's also easy for me to lose it. This isn't something I usually play around with.

But I trust Cassidy. She could tell me no. I kind of want her to tell me no.

She keeps me waiting.

"I don't know . . . you've been good, maybe you've earned it."

My breathing shallows, the tension building. I'm not sure how long I can hold out. Or is she going to take my vibrator away?

"Okay, yes, I think I'd like to see that. Come for me." She leans closer, fucking me carefully but firmly with the Pink Lady as my body starts to shake. I wouldn't usually be able to come on command, but I feel it *right there.*

"I'm coming . . . I'm coming. Fuck! I'm coming!" I tell Cassidy as I feel myself tipping over the edge. I rise into the touch of the dildo and my vibrator. My front hole is unoccupied now but feels good, too, sandwiched between the dual pleasures of my ass and my dick.

I turn my vibrator off as my orgasm ebbs, and Cassidy pulls out the cock, but it feels so good I don't quite want to stop. I set the Magic Wand aside and rub my dick between my fingers. Cassidy bends down to give it a little suck before stepping away to wash up, leaving me blindfolded in bed.

When she comes back, she kneels beside my face. I know she's washed her clit, but I still smell her arousal. I find her with my lips, then take her deep into my throat.

"I want to see your eyes," she says, removing the blindfold. I look up at her briefly before squinting my eyes shut again. Our bedroom is lit only by my bedside lamp on its lowest setting, but as I'm adjusting back from being blindfolded, even that is so bright that it seems to flicker, overwhelming my eyes. Cassidy cups a hand between the lamp and my eye, keeping the direct light out of my face. I slowly open my eyes again as I lick and bob on her dick.

"You are so beautiful," she tells me.

She asks if we can rearrange. She lies down beside me, stroking her clit with one hand and fingering her pussy with the other while I gently take her nipple into my mouth.

Soon I'm watching as come spills out over her hand, belly, and pubes. I keep softly licking her nipple until she relaxes with a deep sigh.

We lie there for a few moments, then both head to the bathroom, she to place the sex toys in the sink for later washing and I to take a quick bath to wash off all the lube.

I linger a little bit, relaxing in the hot water. Soon I'll towel off and join my pink lady in bed for the night.

SKIN DEEP

Angela Addams

I fell in love with your passion for hues, your devotion to skin, your creative expressions.

You fell in love with my hills and valleys, my natural landscape, an uncharted canvass.

My body is primed, freshly showered, exfoliated, but not moisturized and I stretch naked on your preferred working space, the harvest table we stumbled upon at an estate sale long ago. The table that had been so battered and bruised that no one else had paid attention to it, but you'd recognized the beauty the moment you saw it.

You'd said, *It's perfect*, in that husky, excited way I love. *A worthy pedestal for my muse.*

I will never forget the way you looked at me in that moment, eyes radiating heat, ideas already swirling in their depths. It was like your world had come together, with me at the center.

My fire, already an inferno, flared brighter. My heart, my soul, my body melted for you.

You haggled a price even though the table was dirt cheap already but, at the time, starving artist was an understatement of reality for you. We brought it to your studio and got to work, testing to make sure it would hold me up no matter what we did on it. And we did a lot those first few times. You were still experimenting, finding your style. I was getting comfortable with becoming inspiration.

The table is draped in white canvas worn soft by years of use and splattered with every color of the world. That, too, is your art, a testimony to your process. You could sell it for hundreds of thousands. Collectors have offered. But you always decline. It's not for sale, if only because it holds our memories. Each stain, each slash of color, each splatter is a story of our love. The evolution of our lives.

You study me now, paint brush in hand and hunger in your eyes, contemplating how I've arched my back, how my tits point up, my nipples hard, aching for a careful stroke. You leave the pose to me, giving me the freedom to determine the landscape. Today I choose to be bold with my knees bent and legs spread wide. You take me in from all angles, your gaze trails heat over my hills, my valleys, my crevasses, creases, and holes. I shiver as everything inside coils tight, my heart thuds hard enough to stagger my breath. I watch you watching me, marveling at how even after ten years of togetherness, partnering in life and art and all the things, you still find me inspiring. My body has changed; your canvass has developed new ridges, bubbled scars, wider plains, and stretch marks, yet that only seems to spark your creativity more.

Even without your mark, your careful strokes and calculated splatters, I know I'm eternally beautiful, a work of art, if only in your eyes.

Decision made, creativity flaring, you set the brush down

then move the rolling cart closer. You'll start with the spray gun. My skin tingles, goosebumps rising, anticipation of the fine mist as it first hits my body like an aphrodisiac.

Sometimes you prime my skin, white, black, whatever you think your canvass needs, but today isn't one of those days. Whatever your plan is, my uneven olive tones are how you want to start.

I close my eyes, tilt my head back, let the tips of my hair brush the tabletop as I rest my weight on my forearms. My chest moves up, my tits out, the air tickles against my goosebumps, making me shiver.

"No peeking." Your voice is rolling thunder against my ear.

I smile but say nothing. We both know this works so well because I have patience and an unrelenting belief in your process. You are the master right here, right now, and I am your medium.

Besides, it's not the finished product that excites me as much as the journey to get there.

Your first caress is long, bold, splitting me down the middle, between my breasts, past my navel. You coat my pussy curls, what few are there, then trail back over your opening stroke. Up, all the way up to my chin. One continuous spray then a beat or two of nothing before you start again, curving along my ribs, down my side, over my hip, up my thigh, then down to my toes. You don't retrace your steps this time and I have to wait long enough to be tempted to open my eyes. What color did you start with? What design have you planned? What will you do next?

I dare not look. Even though the suspense may kill me.

I shudder through my next few breaths, my body quivering as the ache in my nipples grows and the pulse of my clit forces me to grit my teeth. It's always like this at first, starving for you to touch me, impatient for more determined moves, craving your bold strokes. I'm exposed and open to your whims, vulnerable but confident and trembling for your next touch.

Our foreplay can last for hours. Euphoric torture that teases the wisps of pleasure from the deepest hiding places to roll and play and flick and pinch, tingle and rattle along my sensitive skin.

The spray gun is reloaded again and again as you work over body parts. I know this because my ears are attuned to your movements, the sounds of progress, the whispered muttering that isn't quite frustration but is a signal to me that you're slipping into that meditative place you go when you're sinking into your work. You call it your flow. I call it your zone.

What it means is that things are about to get serious.

I let my mind wander as you coat me with your ideas, remembering the first time you brought me to orgasm with your brilliance. I'd had no idea such a thing was possible. That you could satisfy me without pounding, groping, penetrating, or even kissing. That stimulation came in many forms, sensuality an orchestra and you were already, even so young, a maestro. That time, that very first time, no fingers touched my skin, no lips pressed against my flesh, it was all breath and brush, tiny, microscopic strokes and grand sweeping globs and me in my head, wound tight with anticipation, wondering what part of my body you would adorn next.

As the paint dried, bit by bit, and my skin grew tight, you whispered heated words at my earlobe and to my breasts, along the divot of my navel and the creases under my knees. It was an incantation, a plea, bringing your design to life with fevered intensity. You coaxed me so high, coiled me so tight, that when I unfurled, it was shocking and explosive and otherworldly.

I wanted *moremoremoremore.*

The feathered sweep of paint along the underside of my thigh tempts me to open my legs wider, to invite you in where it's warm and wet and throbbing.

But I won't.

Movement will break the spell you're weaving. It will ruin the surprise and I pride myself on holding still. Like a statue, immobile but pliable, waiting for the signal to shift as you need me to, or hold my breath when you work a particularly fickle spot, or flex, flutter, and pulse when the time comes. And it always comes because you never leave me wanting. You never leave me unsatisfied.

You drag a brush firmly around my breast, the paint so abundant that it trickles down my side. You circle a hair-breadth away from my nipple, then move to the other and do the same. It's watered down, the paint, runny and drying quickly. You smudge the delicate space between my ribs, using a sponge like a masseuse until my skin tingles.

I hold my breath as the hard edge of a palette knife sweeps the peaks of my tits. Your breath whooshes across my skin, pulling a tiny gasp when stiff bristles blend the edges of the paint down the slope of one breast. Then you're back again with the knife, swooping down, following the path that your brush just made in bold lines that slice through the color.

I'm dying, dying, dying to see what you're doing.

But now is not the time for breaking rules. Now is the time to turn inward. To coax those smoldering embers, to tease my passion to the brink, so you can have it, swirl it into your creativity, turn it to an inferno.

"My muse," you coo with marbles in your throat, garbled and husky, full of need. "Just a pinch. A little . . . " You groan as the clamps simultaneously seize my nipples. "Pinch."

I jolt, arching higher as my skin screams and a moan slips

past my lips. It's exquisite agony that makes me writhe, my jaw clenched tight as I breathe, *breathe* through the shock.

Something heavy spans the space between my nipples, holding them tight, forcing cleavage as it brings my mounds together. The jiggle of my tits as I ease my back down again makes the sting all the more real.

The process is always worth the final result.

I want to see what weighs against my nipples. What the clamps are holding up. I clench my eyes tight, letting the temptation pass just as the bite of the clamps slides into a throbbing burn.

You have already moved on. Stroking along my hip, smoothing paint in swirls that calms my thundering heart. Time is running, minutes zooming, you will not torment me for longer than you must.

I hang on with little fires alive over my skin and sink deep into erogenous zones you taught me existed.

The curves of my asscheeks.

The arches of my feet.

The hollow at the base of my throat.

My eyelids, cheeks, and chin.

Your brush strokes caress me.

Your palate knife scrapes hard edges and firm lines.

Your tools: sponges, feathers, mossy textures, and twigs. Things you've collected or created, all used to shape your vision and stoke my flames.

I clench and unclench my pussy, matching your movements over my skin. The pulse between my legs sends lightning bolts over my body, every nerve ending connected.

I imagine layers and textures, bold strokes and vivid color.

What will it be this time? Animal? Nature? Urban decay? What has your mind conjured with my legs spread and my tits leashed together? A stunning goddess? A gnarled tree? Something abstract that looks like the night sky full of pulsating stars but could also be a city brimming with action and adventure and life?

You've turned me into many things over the years. A masterpiece every time.

You work with manic speed. You're all over me, too fast to follow, but it doesn't matter because I'm in my head with every stroke and dab and scrape. Each second brings me closer to release. My skin grows tight. Your hot, moist breath sends shivers through my pussy, like you're penetrating me soul deep as much as you are skin deep.

"Don't move," you whisper growl. "Almost there."

You rake my flesh with something firm, prickles ping in unison and you scratch an itch I didn't know I had.

That alone could make me come.

You tickle beneath my chin with petal soft flutters.

"This right here," you purr, "will be my undoing."

I hear the hungry ache in your voice. It echoes mine.

You want to kiss me.

But you won't break the spell.

You move tenderly, reverently, pausing long enough to caress and worship, minute marks to add the finest details.

"Beautiful, beautiful, beautiful." Your finishing mantra. "My love, we're so close . . . so close."

I hold my breath and stifle the urge to squeeze my legs shut and rock into the rush of completion.

The last stroke is never what I expect it to be.

You brush something ever so slightly against my clamped nipples and, as I hiss my held breath, while pain wracks my tits like daggers plunging down, the shutter click of your camera echoes in my ears.

I picture you staring at me through your lens, click, click, clicking at multiple angles, heights, distances, catching just the right view for your creation to be fully realized.

My skin burns, tight as the paint dries. My nipples ache. My muscles spasm, finally at the breaking point of exhaustion.

I need . . . just a little . . . bit . . . more.

"Do you feel me?" Your voice is almost too soft to hear. "Do you feel my intention? My spark? Do you feel me, love?"

"Yes."

I want to move. To roll my hips and arch until the clamps pull so hard that I scream.

"We're so close, my muse."

I'm so close.

My clit pulses to the beat of my heart. Thudding against the coil of desire that winds ever tighter.

"Not long now." Your voice comes from between my legs. Your breath cascades over my inner thighs.

The coil snaps. The throbbing ratchets and in a flash you're releasing the clamps and an earthquake shudders over my body. My voice is trapped in my throat, a scream stuck as vibrations roll up, down, over.

You scoop me up, not caring now about the paint, only how my body rocks with the never-ending rush of endorphins.

The shower is huge and already steaming when you carry me in. The water hits in a torrent, cascading over my head from above, soothing the burn of my nipples, sluicing the paint from my skin so it can breathe again, adding a harmonious sensation so I pulse on and on and on. Sparks flash behind my eyelids to the tempo of pleasure pulses. My body clenches and unclenches.

You set me down on wobbly legs, holding me around the waist as you tenderly cleanse your hard work from my skin. There's love in your hands as you lather soap into my flesh.

The echo of my climax vibrates through my body and my mind slowly floats back to you.

You bundle me in a terry cloth robe, then carry my noodle limbs to the couch in your studio. I'm a clean slate once again and eager to see the photos, but opening my eyes and keeping them open is a challenge. I'm so deliciously satiated that I could sleep for hours.

The images are loading on the wide-screen TV that's mounted above the fireplace. I curl into you, nuzzle against your chest, and peek at the screen through squinty eyes. Cradled in your arms and cocooned by your artistic pride, the culmination of your energy oozes into me, keeping me warm.

"You never cease to amaze me," you say as you slip a tendril of hair from my face then kiss the tip of my nose. "Look at what you inspired me to do."

Vivid color takes over the screen, deep brown, black, green, gradients that tumble into one another and transform me from hills and valleys, cervices and creases, scars and stretch marks to a masterpiece.

An endangered space, often overlooked, mostly forgotten, but cherished by you.

"Beautiful," you murmur, your eyes on me.

I sigh happily, my eyes glued to the screen.

"Yes," I agree. "Beautiful."

EVICTION NOTICE

Vix Hille

"Remember this? I can't believe I ever had my hair like that."

I glanced at the picture, taking it from his outstretched hand. I couldn't stop myself from laughing. It truly was a horrid haircut. But it was the nineties. Everyone had bad hair back then. Or so we told ourselves.

"I don't know, Mitch. I kinda like it. And if memory serves, I gave you that haircut."

He stared at the picture for a moment before throwing it into a shoebox full of other snaps from the past.

"Yup, that's right. Clearly, after a few too many, Jane," he said with a grin.

"You agreed to it. So whose fault is it really?"

He got up from the floor and ran a hand through my hair as he walked to the kitchen to retrieve another bottle of wine. Our place was in shambles. Years of nonsense and detritus filled every available space on the floor. Ten years' worth of crap that we'd managed to jam into the two-bedroom apartment I'd rented without ever setting foot in the place. The bathroom door was still off the hinges, despite talking to the super about it every month for three years. Two tiles were missing from the kitchen floor, and another was barely hanging on. Mildew grew in the shower stall, no matter how hard we tried to keep it at bay. Plus, the window in the bedroom was drafty and creaky. We'd made a bet that one day it would eventually fall out onto the sidewalk below, but so far, it had never come to pass.

It really didn't come as much of a shock when our lousy landlord finally sent the letter informing us that our time in his charming building was about to end. Part of me was thankful for the push. We'd grown so used to living with all the problems. We'd kept saying we'd find another place, but it never happened. Earlier that year, after a long talk, we ended the conversation about moving on with a plan to stick it out for a while longer, another six months, maybe. Mostly because the rent was so cheap. Now we had twenty-two more days to find a new place to live. A task we hadn't actually gotten to yet. Waiting for a new place to fall into our laps hadn't been doing us much good, so I'd bitten the bullet and scheduled a few visits to new apartments for the weekend.

Now, the task of culling our monstrous pile of stuff was priority one. It seemed easy enough. Just get rid of some of the crap, so moving wouldn't be such a chore. However, once we started going through the boxes and bins that contained our past, it became clear that our sentimental sides were far too overdeveloped. Even now, with some progress made, each picture and trinket caused us to pause and reflect, reminiscing about the event in question. All the trips down memory lane were amazing, but it was starting to take up a lot of time. At the rate we were going, we'd never be done in time to move. And the last thing either of us wanted was to haul shit we didn't need into a shiny new place. Our current clutter-laden existence seemed to match well with our deteriorating surroundings. In order to start fresh, we had to throw some things away.

It was a task that proved to be more monumental than either of us had anticipated. Every time I picked up a useless piece of the past, I knew I should shove it into the black trash bag that sat next to me. Instead, I fought with my logical brain for a way to keep it, a way to justify its existence in our new lives. Mitch was a bit more pragmatic, his garbage bag pile already up to an impressive three. Each one was stuffed so full it looked like it would break open at any moment. Mine sat pitifully half empty, begging for more junk.

Mitch returned with the wine, pouring it into the two mismatched cups we'd chosen thinking we'd throw them out before we moved on. As he filled the silly cartoon-covered glass with more merlot, I thought about how hard it would be to toss it away.

"I see you're not making much progress, Jane."

He nodded toward my bag before plunking down on the floor, pulling a box of God knows what closer to him. As he pulled the lid off, he immediately started tossing the papers, without even looking at them.

"I know. This is difficult. I mean, how am I supposed to know if I'll ever need this stuff again? What if we move and all of a sudden, out of nowhere, we need an old copy of *National Geographic* for something, and I threw them all away?"

He shook his head before sipping his wine from a mug shaped like a football.

"Why would we ever need a magazine from the eighties that we dragged here from your childhood home for absolutely no reason?"

His smirk should have made me mad, but it didn't.

"That's just it. I know, in my head, we wouldn't. But for some reason, the thought of tossing everything and starting again is making me twitchy."

"We don't have to toss everything. Just some of it. I mean, Jesus, how we managed to accumulate this much junk is beyond me. I don't remember what half this stuff is."

"We should have never started opening the boxes. We just should have tossed them without all this . . . examination. It would have been so much easier."

"Agreed."

I shoved a few things into the trash bag before downing most of the wine in my glass. Looking around at the mess, I shook my head and stood up.

"I need a break, Mitch. I can't deal with this stuff right now."

He looked up at me with his shaggy hair and his smudged glasses. He was so damn cute.

"Okay. What do you want to do?"

I knew I should just sit back down and keep working. There was no time for my mini-breakdown. We didn't have the luxury of putting off our move. The deadline for our departure was barreling down at us. My mind just couldn't focus on the practical for another moment. I looked over my shoulder across the disaster that was our apartment and an idea snapped into clarity.

"Something we've been talking about doing since we moved in. Get up."

"Okay."

Mitch scrambled to his feet and followed me on the short walk to the kitchen. He put his hands on his hips and surveyed the space.

"You want to start getting rid of the old pots?"

I shook my head and perched myself on the counter's edge, the whole thing groaning underneath me. I worried for a moment it might collapse under my weight, but it was a chance I was willing to take. Mitch smiled as he stepped in front of me.

"The perfect height," he said, wrapping his arms around my back.

"Yup. And yet we've never, in ten years, taken advantage of that fact. Seems a shame, doesn't it?"

Mitch looked around for a moment before kissing my forehead.

"I thought we agreed the kitchen was too gross to fuck in."

"We did. But this might be our last chance. Don't you think we owe it to ourselves and to this sad little kitchen to send it out with a bang?"

"The only thing we owe this kitchen is a sledgehammer."

"Just work with me on this. I want you. Now. Right here in this kitchen."

Mitch raised his eyebrows and I thought for a moment he might protest further. Instead, he pulled his ratty T-shirt over his head and tossed it aside. His hands went to either side of my face and he kissed me hard.

"Okay. When you put it like that."

He yanked my shirt over my head. His calloused fingertips danced over my nipples, which hardened quickly under his touch. When his mouth closed around one, I let my head fall back and my hands wind through his hair. His tongue always felt like magic, but this time, each delicious circle he traced made another ounce of stress disappear from my body. The thoughts of moving, throwing things away, leaving things behind were gone, replaced by the gentle strafe of his teeth against my nipple. I eased my thighs apart and his hands fumbled trying to get my leggings off. My butt nearly slipped off the counter as my panties joined the pile of clothing that was masking a pile of old dishes.

I reached out to open his cargo shorts, but he stopped me, dropping to his knees in front of me.

"In a minute, Jane."

My thighs were spread even wider, my butt resting right on the edge of the counter. Once again, it creaked at my weight, but I ignored it. Mitch's tongue squirming on my clit had a lot to do with my ability to tune it all out. If it all collapsed underneath me, it would be worth it. I pulled his hair a bit harder as he laved my most sensitive flesh over and over. His hands pressed my legs higher, until my heels were resting on the countertop. Mitch always knew just how to touch me, how to make my blood boil and clear my head of all other thoughts.

His finger slipped inside me, plunging in and out slowly, making me moan. My eyes closed to all the clutter, all the non-sense surrounding us, and focused on the pleasure Mitch was giving me. This was exactly what I needed. I wished I thought of it sooner. With a long, looping sweep of his tongue, Mitch stood up and smiled, kissing me, my taste all over his lips. His cargo shorts were long gone, his hard cock standing at attention. I wrapped my fist around it, stroking its length.

"I want you inside me," I said, breathlessly.

His hands went under my ass, hitching me forward until I felt the head of his dick sliding over my wet pussy. I tried to urge him on, move my hips to get him inside me, but he remained elusive. My arms were around his neck, his lips and teeth moving over my neck.

"Please, Mitch."

Before I could get another word out, he thrust inside me, taking his sweet time, letting me feel every inch. My legs went around his back as if on instinct, his skin warm against mine. His fingers dug into me, his urgency undercut by the lazy pace of his strokes. I could hear his breath in my ear, his soft groans punctuating each roll of his hips.

"Fuck, you feel so good, Jane."

I wanted to answer, but there were no words. My mind wasn't functioning properly anymore. He'd managed to short-circuit everything but my need for him. I hung onto him for dear life; I swore I could feel the counter moving beneath me. The old Formica-covered plywood shook and whined, the pressure almost more than any of us could bear.

"Mitch, I'm so close."

His hands swept through my hair, holding it in both hands as he kissed me, his pace increasing, our bodies moving together in perfect rhythm. Our eyes locked and I knew I couldn't last another second. My pussy clenched around his cock, my toes curling as my legs locked behind his back.

"Oh, fuck. Yes!"

My body shook along with the counter, my orgasm crashing through me with more force than I anticipated. My moans rang against our walls and high ceilings, echoing back as Mitch started to growl, his hips stuttering as he came inside me.

Everything got quiet, our sweaty bodies still entangled, Mitch's tired body slumped against me. Slowly, we pulled apart, and I gingerly got down from the counter, my knees still a bit weak as I stood. Mitch kissed me and smiled, his eyes sparkling.

"So, do you feel better now, Jane?"

I nodded before I spoke, my throat feeling too dry to speak.

"I do. I feel much better."

"Good. Does that mean we can get back to work on the apartment?"

I sighed, letting him pull me close, into his strong arms.

"I guess. I was kind of hoping we could forget about our junk for the day."

"You know we can't do that, Jane. There's too much to do."

I sighed again and ran my hand over his chest. I knew he was right, but I wasn't ready to leave our little fantasy world just yet.

As ugly as our little kitchen was, it had become a respite, one I wasn't ready to relinquish.

"Fine. If you insist. But, I'm going to need a lot more wine to get through all this."

"Okay. Whatever it takes to get you to get something done." We padded down the hall to our undersized bathroom to get cleaned up. I stared at Mitch in the mirror as he turned the taps on, splashing his face with water. After we finished up and got dressed, we settled back to our spots on the floor, picking up where we left off. After my mind was clear, I was able to accomplish more than ever, my garbage bag pile starting to rival Mitch's. As the hours ticked by, the thought of leaving our ratty little place behind was starting to feel better and better. I stood up to get another bottle of wine and something for the two of us to eat.

Returning with popcorn and a bottle of red we'd received as an anniversary present two years before; Mitch jettisoned another box out of the way. We got up off the floor and flopped on the couch, no longer bothering to drink the wine out of our cheesy cups, choosing instead to take pulls right from the bottle.

"I'm proud of us, Jane. We're finally moving out of this hell-hole and onto bigger and better things."

"Me too. I never thought we'd get out of this place alive. I thought for sure that counter was going to give way."

Mitch laughed, taking the bottle from my hands and drinking a long sip.

He ran his thumb over my cheek, sweeping my hair aside before giving me a soft kiss.

"You know, we also never had sex in the spare bedroom, Jane."

He wiggled his eyebrows in a way I hadn't seen him do in a long time. I thought about his words, letting the wine fill my body with warmth.

"Are you sure about that? I seem to recall one night, about five years ago, where we talked about this very thing."

He shook his head and moved a bit closer to me on the couch.

"We talked about it, but we never did it."

I picked up the wine bottle and found it empty. Kissing him, I moved gently into his lap.

"Well, I guess we know what we're doing tomorrow night."

LAVENDER
TEA BREAD

SJ Sweet Bread

Content/trigger warnings: dissociation, emotional flashback, daddy/slut language, demi boy main character, queer masc lover.

My hands are on the kitchen counter, flatly fanned open, attempting to hold myself up. But behind me his flour-caked hands steady my hips, pressing firmly into my softness. Around us there is the chaotic mess of batter, sugar, sticky glass mixing bowls, teal whisks, measuring cups, and spoons, where sweet cream runs down their silver necks, calling out to be licked.

In a tight fist, he has my dress pulled up. The dress does not confuse him. My body is girl, but he knows that there is a part of me that is boy. The other parts, the body parts, more girl, the way the world sees it, but with him, I do not need to continue to explain this. Our bodies learned from each other, a little rocky at first, but found how we could fit together perfectly. Like now, as his hands find comfort in my doughy curves.

"Closer?" he asks, even though we are pretty close already. He wants to be lost in us, too. I push my ass back against the hardness in his jeans, and his index fingers loop under the sides of my panties. The gentle tug sends ripples through me, as I feel my panties drop like sugar on the floor. "Clos-*er*," he says again, pulling me toward him as he does. Skin on warm denim. I respond with a whimper, one he has heard many times before, one dripping with desperate desire.

"I've missed you, baby," he says.

I turn toward him. "I missed you, too," I say, and he places his mouth on mine. There is urgency, remembering how the other moves. His tongue slips in first, testing the pace, eager when I allow him to enter.

"Give me your tongue," he breathes, and sucks and tastes me. The heat between us rises, quickening, finding more of each other, moans escaping both of us, interchanging spit, the edges of our lips wet. We pull back only to take a breath.

Then his mouth moves down my collarbone, bites into my shoulder, discovers the perfect pressure. I am soon met with a trail of slow kisses down where he had left his mark.

We have forgotten the oven from baking our creation earlier and now we can't distinguish the heat in the kitchen from our own. From the time I picked him up from the airport, we were hungry, and we wanted something to do with our hands, which led us to try a lavender tea bread recipe with the leftover lavender flowers we kept for spells.

When we met we bonded over being witches and found comfort in the kitchen. It set a warmth within us, understanding that baking was more than leisure; it was a necessity.

We boiled almond milk (him, lactose intolerant; me, repulsed by regular milk), letting the lavender flowers steep. The smell was rich and warm as we exchanged kisses in between. The butter, sugar, and eggs were mixed until creamy. Then we blended the flour, baking powder, and salt. In another bowl, we let the three pieces combine, then poured the mixture into a pink-tinted, flower-embossed glass loaf pan, baked for an hour, and drizzled it with a lemon-flavored white glaze. The top layer of the golden-colored bread was thick with translucent frosting. We grabbed a bite with our fingers, soft and sweet in the center, letting the lavender stick to the tips of our tongues. We've been letting it cool ever since.

But we have chosen to ignore the oven, and somehow traveled to the other side of the kitchen, a great talent for both of us as my panties are lopsided around my ankles. He pins me to the cabinet and crosses my arms over my head against the wooden cabinet. And then he is on his knees, my cunt inches from his face.

He begins kissing and sucking my inner thighs, leaving what I imagine to be little magenta mementos all over me, the same ones he has left on me before. The memory of what that looks like sends gentle waves through me. He follows it with a firm squeeze on my ass that drives me forward, closer to his lips.

"Tell me what you want," he says in a hot whisper that touches the hairs on my pussy. It's somehow both a statement and a question. I open my mouth, but nothing comes out. Another squeeze. I rock forward, grinding against him. "Hmm?" he asks. And still, the only sound is my loud panting.

I've had the same fantasy for a while now, but it's been difficult to say it out loud. The word dances on the edge of my tongue, threatens to bite for air to breathe.

When we first started talking a few months ago, I shared with him what I want—what I want to call him, what *I* want to be called. But to speak it during moments such as this would be to let it exist, to form into something that could be questioned and vilified.

"Hey," he says to me now, standing up to meet my face. He tenderly caresses the sides of my thighs. "It's okay. *I'm* okay." This lets me know that *we're* okay. I want to tell him what I want, just as easily as he tells me. To command my body to take up space just as lovingly as he holds space for himself and me. Slowly, the weight of the want releases from in my chest.

I open my mouth again, nothing at first, and then, "I want to be your little slut . . . " I say, then hesitate, fear clawing back inside me. " . . . daddy," I finish, my voice so low that even I can barely hear it. The last word demands attention, craves to claim all the air around us.

"Say it again," he says, a tease in his voice. He kisses me— the taste of want.

I smile. Boldness finds me. "I want you to *fuck* me, daddy."

"How? You want daddy's mouth?" he asks.

Yes, I say to myself. Then the courage again. "Yes . . . yes. Yes."

"Yes, what?"

"Yes, daddy," I say, running my hands through his jet-black hair.

He gives a short laugh, one that tells me he's satisfied with that response. "That's daddy's good slut." He moves his lips smoothly from my chest to my belly, his tongue warm and soothing. I ease into it, close my eyes, and let the feeling guide me. I lean back against the cabinet, find my way to the floor. Then one, two fingers. He discovers a dreamy rhythm until he melts inside me. Back and forth gently, letting the wetness cling onto his fingers—a web of juices from me to him. He knows that I don't want a lot of attention on my clit, the intensity too much to bear. So he explores the rest of me, bringing his tongue to the center, thick and cool. He moves from there to my hood, flicking at my folds, slurping at my sopping pussy.

I can hear the sound of me as he continues. The only sound in the kitchen except for my moans. My hand fits nicely in his hair, the motion of his head nodding within me. He groans as he gives skillful sloppy kisses against my lips and thighs.

I begin to disappear, but not in the way where I'm gone. I'm here, and it is just his mouth. A voice tries to take me away, but I ignore it—and bring myself back. Let there only be hips, as I grind against him. His lips so deep inside me that it is just his eyes showing, closed, and he has disappeared, too, into a state of luscious bliss.

And we could both stay like this, but then he is sucking me, like I'm a straw, trying to savor every last drop, and I can't stay here. I'm moving on to whatever comes after heaven. The feeling after you've eaten something delicious, and you want more. I let myself be in it, surrender to the delightful enchantment he has me under. There is nothing to hold without bringing it with me. I am quaking beneath him, and all I can utter is a shout of, "Fuuck," but it comes out as a satisfying fizz. Then I am falling, floating, back to the floor, him wet with me, his chin on my tummy.

We both lay on the cold floor with our sweaty backs, still dusted with our adventurous baking mess. He scoots closer to me, so his head is on my chest. I imagine that he is listening to my heart, paying attention to how it beats, loving that he was the one to make it go faster and the one to slow it down evenly.

Then the reality sinks in, tries to cut the lavender air that surrounds us.

It begins in my throat, where it often starts. The pleasure I received from his hands earlier now feels like I am being tugged at from the inside. But beside me, he is kind, content. It is only me, drifting away from him as the voices in my head become my own. *Slut. Slut. Slut. His mouth was not yours.*

I know that I am lying beside him, now on this floor with our mess. But that is another version of me, a version who forgets the child who often finds their way to the surface. The boy, who is tired of being buried. And as I feel myself become that child again, the body next to me shifts.

His finger moves one of my braids from my forehead, and he says, "Where are you, my love?"

It all brings me back to here, because here I am, with him, on this floor, full of our messes. I breathe in, breathe out. Calmness wades through the thickness. I am here. On this floor. There is the lavender tea bread, still warm, covered in tin foil. We made it together. The clock on the wall ticks, letting me know that time exists, and it is moving forward. I don't even realize the perspiration on my forehead until his hand touches and wipes it off, without saying anything. He knows, where I went, where I've gone, and that I've returned, with him, with me.

And now, I can speak. "I'm here," I say, my voice small, but he can hear it.

"Good," he says, kissing my forehead, and we help each other off the floor. "Let's clean up."

OUT OF ORBIT

R. Magdalen

There was a hiss of gas escaping as the cover of the stasis pod opened. Cap was disoriented for a moment. It took time to acclimate after such a long period. She sat up slowly and massaged her aching limbs and removed the breathing tube from her nose and the IV from her arm. Her neck cracked audibly. Despite the fact that the interior of the pod was supposed to offer perfect humidity, her mouth felt like sand and she fumbled for the bottle of water she kept nearby. The water tasted like pure beauty.

Cap had a routine after a stasis period. She always set the wake-up protocols for a couple of hours before she had to check in with Devin, her first mate, who had been in charge of things for the last month-long rotation. It took at least that long to get her head on straight. Water first. Then a whole lot of stretching. Your body wasn't supposed to age or change at all during a stasis sleep, but Cap's joints were getting older anyway. She climbed sluggishly out of her pod and started a stretching video on a screen on the wall. More audible pops from her joints. She'd hit the gym soon, she promised herself.

One last step and she would start to feel more alive. She mixed hot water with a nutrient-enhanced, mushroom-based powder flavored with bitterness and light caramel notes in an old mug from Earth labeled "Coffee." It was more delicious than the concoction deserved to be, but everything tasted better after stasis. She was ready for her messages.

There were Devin's ship logs to go through, but nothing urgent. Had anything truly terrible happened, she would have been woken up before the alarm. It looked like everyone had done their job well, and they were on schedule. No surprises there. Devin was competent, if not overly conscientious. The logs could wait.

They would be arriving at Griffin Station in a few weeks to drop off cargo, pick up cargo and maybe a few passengers, and everyone would get a much-needed bit of shore leave. She had the budget to hire another crew member, as well, and there were already some resumes among the messages. Those could wait, too. There was something else she needed to see. There it was. Three messages. She pressed the screen harder than necessary.

"Hey, baby. I know you're in stasis, but I love the thought of you waking up to a little bit of me." There was Mel's beautiful face, absolutely the best thing to wake up to. Cap traced Mel's perfect, deep brown cheekbones, leaving a smudge on the screen. Her hair was gray and cut closely in stark, perfect lines that contrasted with the darkness of her skin. It had been black when they last saw each other in person. Mel had been a lot younger than Cap back then. Now, after so much time, time at faster-than-light speeds, and time in stasis, she was catching up. "Things are going great these days. This asteroid has so many interesting fossils. It's like every layer we uncover has some kind of life from a different part of the universe. It looks like I'll be able to officially name some new proto-life forms! I'm attaching the paper, but you don't have to read it. I'm the lead author on this one though.

"Oh! And we got a load of supplies, and there was this package from you! I figured I'd unwrap it on camera. Oooo, look at this!" Mel unwrapped a little notebook made out of real tree paper, exported from Earth. "I love it, baby! That's so sweet of you!" Cap smiled. It hadn't been easy to arrange. There was a note inside, but Mel hadn't seen it yet.

"Paul sends you his love." Cap felt a brief prickle at the mention of her metamour, but it passed. She was glad Mel had support, glad she had company on her extended research mission to Bennu. Mel would hate it if she was jealous. It wasn't Paul who was keeping them so far away from each other. It was fucking science. "He's having fun cataloging minerals, as usual. Nobody is mining Bennu yet, but they're going to have to before it gets blown to bits." The last part sounded wistful.

"Call me when you're up. Your itinerary says you're going to be at Griffin, and that should be close enough for us to get a com-link going. We could talk . . . or have a date! I love you. Oh, and here!" Mel could not send a message without a wink and a flash of her gorgeous breasts. Cap laughed, but paused the recording to stare at them. Mel's beauty was undeniable, but it was so bound up in her personality, her humor . . . Cap took a moment to imagine what those titties smelled like, how they felt in her hands. That feeling was years away in either direction. The message was dated weeks ago, so Cap checked the computer. They could be in range in four days.

Two more messages.

"I know you just saw my tits. Here's my ass!" Cap smiled at

that image, too. She paused the video to stare again and considered jerking off, but she still felt like crap from stasis. The message could go in an archive she kept of such things.

The final message was dated a week later and included a whole file of artfully posed photographs to look at when she felt better. Still so hot for each other after so many years. She had to admit it was probably because of the distance that they'd been "together" that long rather than despite it. She put the photos in the spank bank with the videos.

She studied her own face on the screen before recording a message for Mel. She looked like shit. Her skin was pale and clammy and her thick auburn hair desperately needed a cut, despite the fact that hair wasn't supposed to grow in stasis. A change of clothes needed to happen as well. Luckily, the captain's quarters came with its own bathroom situation. She clipped her hair into a crisp fade, and added some eyeliner that helped her look a little less like death. A good camera angle and a touch of pink filter wouldn't hurt either. She checked herself again, bared her canines in what she hoped was a sexy smile, and summoned her butch swagger for the call.

"Mel! You know your face is the best thing to wake up to! No, make that your titties. And that video of your ass . . . " She gestured a chef's kiss. "I'm sending some potential time slots. It's been too long, sweetheart. We're spending a few weeks at Griffin, so we can spend some real time together while you're in range. Or, you know what I mean . . . anyway, I'll send you a longer message later. I gotta get to work. I love you, babe."

Cap finished her beverage and headed to the main deck of the ship to check in with her crew. Devin was clearly eager to give a briefing.

"Good morning, Captain," she said brightly. She stood at attention, unnecessarily. "We experienced thirty-seven small collisions while you were in stasis. Twenty-three of them required repair. Eddie is finishing up the last one, but we should see smooth sailing until Griffin."

"Thank you, Devin," said Cap. "You can relax. Uh, at ease."

"Yes, Captain," Devin said. "I also asked the crew to submit supply requests at least two weeks before arrival. And I have an initial shore leave schedule for your approval. We are all very excited to see the station, sir." Cap glanced at the schedule on her console and made a few adjustments. She'd been there before. While she looked forward to walking around in higher gravity and maybe having a smoke, shore leave was not as important as having a date with Mel. Or as many dates as possible.

"Oh, thank you, Captain," said Devin, seeing her shore leave time double on her own console.

"You deserve it, Devin. And you can stay in the captain's suite when I'm not giving interviews."

The next four days were filled with maintenance tasks and preparation for arrival at the space station. Working on her own ship . . . well, a ship under her own command, although it didn't exactly belong to her, had been her lifelong dream. She loved it. Whipping around the solar system, even the occasional long haul. She never knew where she might end up going next or who she might meet. There were also the boring tasks, though, that paid the bills. All of the twelve passengers would be disembarking on Griffin, as well as about twenty shipping containers of cargo. More of both would have to be arranged. Supply inventory, shore leave schedules, customs forms had all been done in advance during the long, uneventful journey from their last stop.

Cap kept everything pretty close to the vest when it came to her crew. None of them knew anything about her personal life. She arranged the date for a time when as few people as possible were on the ship, but she'd be off-duty, not giving a reason, but making it very clear she could not be disturbed.

It was Mel who had bought the haptic suits to add a little spice to this extremely long and extremely distant phase of their relationship. They used them whenever they were close enough for satellites to relay a real-time connection. It had all been a hard sell for Cap, living without her, but the asteroid Bennu's rotation was so fast that you had to have special inner ear and brain modifications to spend any time there without throwing up until you died, so in-person visits were a major health risk. They still talked about retiring together someday, though, when the research was over.

"Babe, are you there?" The screen switched over to Mel's beautiful face and a bit of static that went away quickly.

"Yes! We're docked at Griffin."

"Wow! What's it like?" Griffin Station was the furthest Earth station from the sun, and the closest place to Earth that was frequented by people from other solar systems. "I've always wanted to see it."

"Actually, I haven't been off the ship. I wanted some time with you first."

"Oh, babe, thank you! Let's get these things connected. I want to feel you."

The suits took a minute to connect, and both women had to make some small adjustments. They were skintight and metallic, and showed every fold, crevice, and roll of fat, but the details were a bit obscured. Cap needed the visor to make sense of the input from the suit. She had to see Mel touch her arm for it to feel like Mel. It was disorienting for the first five or ten minutes. They could choose a background, and an image of the other person appeared in front of them. Tonight, Cap chose a black void, but lit their bodies with a circle of candles. Suddenly, there was Mel, floating naked slightly above her. The ship was using the gravity system of the space station, but Mel's had no gravity at all. She opened her arms to Cap like an angel from on high and sank into a hug.

The haptic suits detected and created pressure and vibration, so the two women could feel the pressure of the hug, and the movements of the other person in real time, which corresponded to what they could see on their visors. You couldn't feel weight, or the smoothness of skin, but there was some amount of temperature change and vibration. It was like being touched through thick clothing.

Still, Cap couldn't keep her hands off Mel once she started. She rubbed Mel's shoulders and back, and moved down to one of her favorite parts of Mel's body. Mel's plump, juicy ass had gotten bigger and rounder with age, and Cap needed time to reacquaint herself. She began massaging each asscheek in circles, taking her time, feeling the firm fat move beneath her hands. Mel's hands moved to her shoulders.

"Mmmm. It feels so good just to be with you."

"Yesss," Cap answered, too focused on her lover's ass to articulate a better response. She moved her hands over Mel's wide hips like a meditation, then her belly and then her breasts. She could feel how they moved under her hands, round and malleable. She longed to put them in her mouth and suck them but that technology had yet to be invented. Nothing stood in the way of her teasing Mel's nipples, though, even pinching them slightly, which delighted her.

This kind of sex was limited in many ways, but one major advantage was the suits' vibration feature, which was activated by a certain movement of the fingers. Pinching and rubbing Mel's huge, beautiful nipples turned into rolling them between Cap's gloved fingers, which turned into deep, pulsing vibes. Mel leaned back in her enjoyment and the screen-in-screen on Cap's visor showed Mel's wide smile and closed eyes. She was such a beautiful woman. Her dark skin glowed golden in the candlelight on the display, more illuminated in silver on camera. Mel's legs parted in front of Cap, her suit-covered vulva poised and wanting.

However, Cap wasn't one to rush things, even after waiting six months since their last session. She wanted to tease and pleasure her lover's whole body, so she caressed and squeezed Mel's belly and sides, and slathered more intense attention on her hips and ass. Cap massaged and vibrated trails down Mel's body, stopping at known erogenous zones and experimenting with new ones, once even fixating on the back of Mel's knee, stroking and vibrating until Mel came with a shiver. Then Cap was lost again in the wonders of Mel's hips and thighs, coming so close to the needy vulva.

"Baby, you're teasing me. I want you."

"You have me. Right now. I want to get my fill of you and this sexy body of yours. So I'm going to drag this out and savor every bit of it."

By now they were both wet, another sensation that couldn't be shared by the suits. Cap's body hadn't ever really accepted the limitations of the situation, and she viscerally craved the taste and smell of Mel's pussy. She said as much, and Mel replied with a passionate moan. She rubbed her thumbs under the curve of Mel's asscheeks, closer and closer to that pussy. When she finally slid her hands between Mel's legs, they both let out a sigh, of connectedness, pleasure, and home. They faced each other and looked into each other's eyes as rendered by the visor's program. Cap tried to hold the rendering's gaze, and squeezed Mel's vulva, gently, and then more firmly.

"This is mine, you know," said Cap, a wolfish grin on her face. She squeezed as hard as the suit allowed and Mel gasped.

"Yes, all of it is yours."

Cap continued squeezing at just the right angle, with just the right intensity, and accelerated slowly, taking time to build up to another orgasm for Mel. It was petting like they'd done on their first date, but soon Mel opened her legs and Cap turned the vibration up and made circles around the place she knew Mel's clit was located. In the visor, Mel's pussy glittered, wet and inviting.

The haptic suits were originally made for military simulations and then perfected for video games, but the inventors were very aware that they would immediately be used for sex and had created several extremely cool devices to cash in on this use of their product.

"Baby, are you ready? Can I have you?"

"Yes, now, please!"

Mel reached for the dildo attachment, gave it a dollop of lube, and put it inside herself. As she attached the base of the dildo to the suit and zipped up, Cap was already thrusting slowly, moving her hips. The dildo stayed in place, but it pulsed and changed thickness in response to Cap's movements, as if there were a weighted ball that moved through the silicone tube until it reached a bulbous head, which tapped Mel's cervix in a way that made her feel like she might gush. The dildo was already large, and when parts of it thickened, Mel felt full, even a little bit stretched.

Cap looked down at her own body through the visor, which now had a penis, and it made her chuckle. It was a novelty, still, but if they were in-person it would be her fist inside Mel, and that thought sent her attention to her own clit. The haptic suit had a vibrator patch just where the dildo would be if it were really attached to her, and with each thrust it gave her clit a wave of thuddy vibration. Watching herself fuck Mel's beautiful pussy on the visor made her clit even more wet and engorged.

It was almost as if she could feel it, the way the vibration was triggered by their bodies, as if the penis was real. Cap kneaded Mel's breasts, moving her hips in time with Mel's delighted sighs until Cap felt herself coming. Mel joined her and they kept fucking through the orgasm, slowed slightly, and then another. After the third, Cap tapped out, tired and overcome. They both knew that Mel could go all night if she wanted to, but her expression was extremely mellow and satisfied.

"Oh, my gods, baby, that was just what I needed."

"Yeah. I love you."

"I love you, too. Hey, do you want to hear more about the fossils we're finding?"

"Yeah, babe. Let me take off this sweaty suit and sit down. Switch to screen?"

Now they sat down and faced each other through monitors, each a little flushed and sweaty.

"I read your paper. It's really fascinating. You are so brilliant. My brilliant girl."

"Seriously? You read it? I'm so glad."

Cap got the entire lowdown on the protopaleontology of a distant asteroid while she changed out of the suit and into pajamas and made a cup of tea. Mel's face when she was explaining her very favorite topic was worth it, worth all the distance, worth all the rare bursts of real-time contact.

"So, what are you going to do on Griffin Station? Anything fun?"

"We're swapping cargo, getting new passengers. I might hire some more crew."

"Maybe someone cute?"

"Nah, I'm not looking. The last thing I need in this role is drama. I've got enough to do. Besides, you're my girl." They both laughed a little at that, Cap perhaps less genuinely.

"So sweet! I hope it all goes well."

"We'll be able to do this a few more times before we're out of range again."

"Absolutely!" There was a beep, and Mel looked at something on her screen. "Listen, I have to go check on some wonky drills on Bennu in a few minutes, but we'll meet up tomorrow, okay? I love you."

"Yeah, tomorrow. Okay. I love you, too. Oh, and Mel?"

"Yes?"

"Tell Paul he better be taking good care of my wife."

"Ha. I will. Bye."

REKINDLING

Austin Worley

When Maira finally closed those marvelous eyes, Earc Mac Toghda couldn't help but sigh. *Oh, thank the gods!* He waited a few more moments, then added a woolen blanket to her cradle. Ancient sorcery protected selkies from even the coldest ocean depths, but he didn't have the slightest clue whether she took after him instead of her mainlander mother.

Better safe than sorry.

Earc rose and stoked the fire before shuffling back to bed, where Arlise greeted him with a sleepy smile. "So?"

"Fast asleep," he answered, joining her beneath the furs.

"Good." She wrapped one arm around him and leaned in close. Close enough he almost drowned in her scent. Lavender. Hints of blade oil. Mint on her breath. Memories of the very first time she'd held him like this left his cock straining against soft wool, and year-old yearnings sharpened as lithe fingers began to trace his bronzed physique. "Fatherhood looks so fetching on you."

Heart aflutter, he tucked a lock of blonde hair behind her scarred ear and pressed a gentle kiss to her lips. Arlise answered with all the ferocity of a gale in autumn, knocking him back against the goose-feather pillows. The tingly aftertaste of mint mouthwash cooled his tongue as slender fingers roamed lower and lower. One swift tug undid his loincloth.

Before his shaft could spring free, she teased the rim of his swollen cockhead. *Sweet Áine!* Earc arched and allowed himself to melt into her embrace until he couldn't remember where she ended and he began. Only when his lungs ached for release did he break away, panting.

Bright blue eyes sparkled in the firelight, and he marveled at the galaxies they held before slipping one hand beneath the hem of her linen shift. "Fatherhood is nothing," Earc whispered, "compared to how lovely motherhood looks on you."

Arlise froze, then snatched her hand away. Almost like his cock burned to the touch. Muscles honed over years hunting terrible monsters and darkest magic bunched up as she crossed her arms and scooted backward. "On second thought, can we not do this tonight?"

Too bewildered to find his tongue, he simply nodded.

"Thank you for understanding, Earc." She kissed him on the cheek, rolled over, and pulled the furs on their bed up under her chin.

But I don't understand anything . . . Echoes of her touch left him slick and twitching as he gazed up at the hides stretched over the whalebone frame of their hut. Waves of emotion roiled his mind. Confusion and concern, boundless desire and more than a little frustration . . . gradually, they all settled into a bone-deep longing. Earc glanced at the remarkable woman slumbering beside him. *How did we come to this?*

Last year, once she'd slain the sea monster plaguing his clan and he'd conquered his fear of heartbreak, they could barely keep their hands off each other. Even after a sleek caravel arrived to fetch her and her shipwrecked comrades, their ardor never faded. Arlise's love letters were so lurid, just thinking about them scorched his cheeks.

Everything changed when she brought their daughter to Quiet Cove.

At first, he'd simply assumed she was exhausted from the long journey and tending a pup alone. But despite a month of rest and a whole colony of selkies eager to help, they hadn't made love once since their reunion.

Does she even want me anymore?

Earc scoffed at himself. Hadn't she snuggled up to him? Hadn't she stripped him naked and stroked him until her hand glistened with his arousal? Of course she wanted him!

So why did a sweet nothing scare her off?

Answers proved more elusive than black pearls, and fearful questions riddled him with self-doubt. By the time the hearth fire burned low, only one thing was certain: their bond suffered from some unspoken wound.

Throat clenched tight, Earc blinked back tears. Losing Arlise . . . he couldn't bear the thought. Not when their future seemed so bright. The Order of Watchers had granted her two years of maternity leave. More time than they'd ever steal on her rare visits between life-or-death missions. Time enough to truly cherish each other. But if they allowed this wound to grow and fester, it would ruin everything.

Gods, what to do?

Memories bubbled up. Memories of how his parents always dealt with their problems. *Best to wash our wounds with words.* They needed somewhere quiet, though. Away from clan and parenthood's constant demands. Somewhere guaranteed to rekindle their romance.

As he bedded down for the night, Earc realized he knew the perfect place.

Waves lapped at his flippers, but Earc galumphed ashore without paying any heed to the cool waters of Quiet Cove. Instead, he tapped power stored in the enchanted sealskin which had transformed him. Sharp teeth chattered. A low hum filled the air. Then everything flared white as magic sculpted flesh and bone back into their natural shapes. Somewhere further inland, a flock of startled songbirds took flight.

Bits of color peeked through the blinding radiance. First the golden-yellow glow of enchantments at work, next puffy clouds parting to reveal a bright blue sky, and finally the dappled cream-and-gray sealskin wrapped around his naked body. An unseasonably warm breeze washed over him, and he savored its caress.

Then magic hummed again further down the beach.

"By the Mother and all Her Prophets," Arlise growled as she wrestled with her borrowed sealskin, "I'll never get used to these things!"

Chuckling, Earc stood and threw his pelt over one shoulder. "Need some help?"

Tanned cheeks paled, and she pulled up the sealskin to hide her nakedness. "No, don't look at me!"

Odd. Hadn't he seen every delightful inch of her body a hundred times already? Before duty parted them, she'd forsaken clothing just like her selkie hosts. Now, she always wore a shift, a loose mainlander dress, or the black-on-white gambeson which marked her as a Knight-Mother in the Order of Watchers. Why such a stark change?

He shook his head. *Mainlanders and their silly notions of modesty.* Nevertheless, Earc obediently averted his gaze and trudged through the sand to a spot just shy of the pine forest which blanketed Ruby Isle. *Perfect!* A wicker basket full of food and mainlander wine, another with bearskin blankets, dry branches and twigs in the fire pit . . . all his secret preparations from yesterday were still in place.

Reaching across his innate connection to the Outerworld—the realm of spirits and magic—Earc conjured heat until the pine needles in the pit burst into flames. Seconds later, a blaze strong enough to fend off any wintry chill roared to life. While he spread out the first blanket, Arlise finished wrapping the sealskin around her torso.

"Now will you finally tell me where we—" Whatever else she meant to say died on the tip of her tongue, and he grinned at the recognition in those sparkling eyes. Bearskin sprawled out where they'd first made love. The basket of bread and cheese and wine sat where she'd stripped for him. Rosy patches blossomed on her chest as she walked past the spot where he first worshipped her with his tongue. "You set all this up by yourself?"

"Not completely." Further along the beach, half-buried in sand and pebbles, lay the empty shell of a sea monster dubbed Carmun. A crab-like horror Arlise had slain singlehandedly, never asking for anything in return. Remembering her selfless courage sent chills down his spine and stirred his cock. Earc shifted uncomfortably. "Selkies aren't the only folk who owe you a debt. When he heard my plan, Old Man Reil loaned me his fishing boat so I could sneak some things across the cove."

Arching an eyebrow, she took a seat on the fur beside him. "And what is this plan?"

"For you and me to enjoy a beautiful day. No fish to catch, no demons to banish, no squalling baby to tend. Who knows? Maybe sparks will fly like the last time both of us were alone on Ruby Isle."

Eyelashes fluttered as she stared at the sea, and her voice crackled with sorrow. "I don't know if we'll ever find that spark again. Everything has changed."

"Everything is always changing."

"But we don't always enjoy those changes." Arlise took a deep breath and rubbed her thumb against the band of pale skin around her ring finger. "What if you don't like the ways I have changed? Physically?"

So that's what this is all about . . .

Tears coursed down suntanned cheeks as she tucked both knees under her chin. "At first, they didn't seem so awful. But . . . it's been four months. *Something* is always sore or swollen or stretched. Sister Bowen taught me some exercises, but my core still feels weaker than ever. My vision went blurry a few times. When the bloody discharge stopped, I hoped my recovery was almost over. Now clumps of my hair are falling out!"

Earc reached up to dry her tears and trace the crinkled burn along her jaw. "Your scars never bothered me, *mo fhíorghra.* Neither will any of these other things."

"My scars aren't even half as hideous as . . . *this.*"

"Remember what I told you when we first kissed?" Bright eyes glittered in the sunlight as he gently lifted her chin. "Nothing about you is hideous."

Thin lips drew into an even thinner line. "How would you know? You haven't seen my naked body in a year!"

"So show me. Please."

For a moment, she hesitated. Then her gaze strayed to the clear bead of arousal glistening at the tip of his cock. A bashful smile danced on her lips as slender fingers reached up to unknot the sealskin. Slowly. Timidly. Tossing the enchanted pelt aside, Arlise scooted back and bared herself to him.

Aye, she was different. Stretchmarks arced across her belly, where both bands of muscle refused to knit back together. At a guess, this faintly pregnant look bothered her the most. Spidery veins, lost muscle definition, hips and thighs gone a little softer . . . all much less obvious. But *none* of those changes mattered. She was still the savior of his clan, the woman he loved, and the mother of his daughter. One year ago on this very beach, she'd accepted him completely. What kind of man would he be if he didn't do the same?

Earc swept a hand down her flank and listened to the stories her scars told.

Beautiful.

The word slipped off the tip of his tongue, and she sniffled before meeting his gaze. "You still think so? Truly?"

"Of course." A gentle push left Arlise propped up on both elbows, and his cock dripped all over the fluffy tuft of hair atop her mound as he leaned in close enough to whisper. "If you need any proof of my feelings, just say the word."

"*Yes.*"

Her scorching kiss caught him off guard. So off-guard he didn't even kiss back at first. A cool, familiar tingle blossomed as their tongues intertwined. Earc groaned into the kiss, then groaned again when she arched her hips. Slick folds glided along the underside of his shaft, slathering their mingled juices from root to swollen cockhead, and he almost burst.

Gods!

Desperate to avoid such an early finish, Earc trailed gentle kisses down, down, down. One brushed an engorged nipple, and she gasped. *Always so sensitive here.* Capturing the tender nub between his lips, he sucked hard and flinched when milk welled up. But what better way to show Arlise how little he cared about the ways her body had changed?

Brushing a thumb against the soft flesh beneath her other

breast, Earc gazed at Arlise. Bright eyes wide, cheeks flushed, pouty lips parted ever so slightly, a low moan rising at the back of her throat . . . the very picture of a goddess. He nipped and suckled and relished her creamy sweetness until his mouth reduced that goddess to a panting mess.

Once he drank his fill of her, more kisses trailed across the gentle swell of her belly, through damp brown tufts, and onto the little pearl nestled amidst her folds. Molten heat washed over him, followed by a medley of aromas. Lavender. Hints of sea salt. Musky feminine arousal. Breathing them deeply, Earc glanced up from her pussy. "Make yourself comfortable, *mo fhíorghra.*"

"Such a tease," Arlise whined as she spread trembling thighs wide and rested them against his shoulders.

"Always."

Instead of returning to her clit, he lapped at the nectar on those glistening folds. Light. Syrupy. A faint metallic tanginess whenever his tongue delved deeper. Such a delicious woman. Sated, he trawled higher and higher.

"Moan for me," she whimpered. Lithe fingers tangled themselves in his unruly hair and tugged hard. Nose smooshed into slick curls, lips around her little pearl, sopping folds against his chin . . . he almost drowned in her juices. "Please."

Vibrations rumbled through her sweet spot as he obeyed.

"*Ohhh,* that's perfect!"

Her praise left his cock drooling onto the fur blanket where he knelt, and part of him yearned to stroke himself. But after a year without any intimacy, Earc knew he couldn't endure even the lightest touch for long. Wouldn't parting her beautiful lower lips and sliding deep inside offer both of them more pleasure in those precious moments?

Tongue fluttering against her clit, he brushed a finger over dewy petals before plumbing her depths. *Gods, she's so wet!*

Even wetter than the first time they made love on this beach. A second finger dipped into her steaming cove, then a third, and she arched as they stroked a bundle of nerves just inside.

"*Earc!*"

Every hair stood on end at the way she lilted his name, her face a mask of beautiful agony etched with desperate desire. Memories from the other night bubbled up, and he scoffed at himself for ever doubting she wanted him.

Earc synchronized his tongue and fingers with each wave rippling against the shore. Whenever they ebbed, he added a moan or sucked on her clit. Then the dance of pleasure began again. Stroke and flutter, moan. Stroke and flutter, suck. Stroke and flutter, moan. On and on until she writhed like a sea serpent.

Wetness smeared from chin to cheekbone and back again as she ground against him. Pinning her down with a strong arm across her pelvis, he drew the little pearl between his lips and sucked hard. Brawny thighs clamped around him like a vise, fingernails clawed at his scalp, and her pale chest flushed strawberry-red.

"Fuck," Arlise mewled as she fondled her breasts. "Fuck!"

Not long now . . . She never cursed unless she teetered on the edge of ecstasy. But instead of finishing her off, he pried himself out from between her legs, sat on his heels, and wiped away her slippery nectar.

Blushing cheeks darkened. "Sorry."

"Don't be, *mo fhíorghra.*" He inched closer and rubbed the crown of his cock against her swollen clit. "When you almost crush my skull like a walnut, I know you're enjoying yourself."

Gazing up at him with lust-lidded eyes, Arlise gripped his shaft and pressed the dripping tip into her pussy. "So many nights alone, dreaming of you, but my fingers couldn't replace your cock. Stop teasing and fuck me."

Muscular legs wrapped around his hips and drove him deeper. Tense, ticklish heat spiraled down his length before melding into the molten heat of slick inner walls. They gasped in unison, and she gasped again when he reached up to knead her breasts. Milk dribbled from the nipple pinched between his fingers.

"Prophets!"

Rings of muscle clenched around him on the downstroke, as if she couldn't bear the emptiness he left behind. As if she needed him stuffing her nice and tight. A flutter filled his chest at the thought. Then her grip loosened, and he thrust so deep his stones tapped against the graceful curve of her ass.

Soon they settled into a steady rhythm. Clench. Stroke. Loosen. Thrust. Over and over until he slumped against her. Their foreheads pressing together, hardened nipples prodding him gently, the adoration in those brilliant blue eyes . . . Earc almost came undone right then and there.

Desperate to satisfy her before himself, he angled each thrust so his cockhead would graze the sweet spot at her entrance. Warm hands cupped his face as she squealed and shuddered. Soft lips wiped the last traces of nectar from his chin with fluttery kisses.

The beat quickened: clench, stroke, loosen, thrust.

One hand reached down between them to circle her clit while the other held him close. Close enough for loose strands of blonde hair to tickle his nose. Then the tempo of their lovemaking shifted again. Faster and faster her rippling walls clutched at his cock. *Sweet Áine!* Orgasmic spasms swept through him from head to toe and back again, pumping her pussy full of warm seed. Teeth nipped his earlobe. When a satisfied moan welled up from somewhere deep within his chest, she muffled his cry with a frantic kiss.

Once the final echoes of their mutual pleasure shuddered through him, Earc eased himself from her channel and flopped onto the fur blanket. Any hint of clouds was gone. Far off across Quiet Cove, pine forests and squat selkie huts crowned the chalk cliffs of Aolchloch. But not even such a beautiful vista could compare to the woman beside him.

Arlise scooted over and rested her head on his shoulder. "I feel like a fool for worrying my body would drive you away."

"Don't." He reached out to trace the rings of black triangles tattooed around her bicep. "When you shrank away from me the other night, I feared you didn't want me anymore."

"Prophets, we almost ruined everything."

"Aye," he whispered. "But at least we cleaned up our own mess."

Her lips spread into a wicked grin as she sat up. "If this is how you clean, I might just spend the next two years in *shambles.*"

"You'll never stay that way for long, though."

She leaned back and parted glistening folds to reveal a pale stream dribbling into the cleft of her ass. "Is that a promise?"

Earc crawled between her legs and answered with his tongue.

MIRIAM, UNDONE

Lou Morgan

Nella Sorensen sashays into the hotel lobby, heels clicking against the polished marble floor. Nella turns heads, body poured into the black cocktail dress she keeps for family weddings and work parties. Without Miriam to hand, she'd tugged the zipper up with the aid of a coat hanger, a mirror, and a prayer. But—even with the acrobatics—Nella has saved time; Miriam would've had her twice before she'd made it out the door.

Nella smiles at the thought, following the gently pulsing music into the bar. There's a scattering of couples, a cluster of suits fresh from the city, and there, on the upper level, Miriam, ensconced among her fellow academics.

She sees it, the moment when Miriam notices her: a frown, then that subtle, wolfish smile. But Nella turns her back on Miriam, strolling to the bar and ordering a mojito. She hoists herself up onto the barstool, slides a ten-pound note across the chrome counter, and waits. The drink isn't half bad, when it comes.

Though she will grudge the London tax until the breath leaves her body, the rum mellows Nella.

Her outfit begins to feel less pantomime, more espionage. Nella doesn't often wear dresses. Mainly to avoid the rigmarole of shaving. All that bare skin: legs, arms, back, décolletage. It usually leaves her feeling exposed, but tonight Nella is invincible.

Or so she tells herself. Nella can't help but start each time she gazes into the mirror, scarcely recognizing this softer version of herself. Curls piled high to conceal her undercut, lips painted plum, contacts instead of chunky frames, she looks . . . almost pretty. One of the suits seems to think so too, for he winks at her reflection.

Nella looks away, stirring the ice cubes with her paper straw. Her eyes dart toward Miriam, sure as a needle finding true north. She sits at the top of her table, head thrown back in laughter.

Miriam is not beautiful, not exactly. She's the kind of woman Djuna Barnes might have described as handsome, with lively brown eyes and a broad mouth. She has a shining cap of hair, trimmed weekly into a precise bob and shaved in at the nape of her neck. The blunt fringe—always a full inch shy of femininity—gives the impression that Miriam is all hard angles. But under the crisp shirts and finely tailored suits, her curves are generous.

Nella had known, the moment she set eyes on her, that Miriam was a lesbian. Though the men around Miriam don't always guess at it, her aesthetic passes for eccentric, amongst the rich and within the halls of the academe. Even if they do not realize what sets Miriam apart, it's clear from the way they lean toward her, vying to win another laugh, that they find Miriam intoxicating.

And Nella sympathizes. She couldn't go three nights without

Miriam in her bed. Spent all afternoon on the train, anticipation building in the pit of her belly as every stop brought her closer to Euston.

The full force of Miriam's confidence bowls her over, even now. *"The key,"* Miriam had once told Nella, *"is in how you hold yourself. Walk into a room as if you own it, and nobody will question your presence.*

"It's more the shade of my skin than how I wear it, that security guards see as the invitation to question," she'd said.

For once Miriam had no comeback. They'd fucked, afterward. First on Miriam's cool marble kitchen counter; again on the stairs, Miriam's tongue darting inside her; and then finally in the bedroom, every nerve aflame. Yet the truth of that difference had hung in the air between them, mingled with the scent of sex. Even as her body melted over Miriam's, deep brown against pale cream, Nella had suspected it was a kind of goodbye.

Miriam had surprised her. "Look, I know that I talk as if I know everything, but, as I made excruciatingly clear downstairs, there's a lot I'm still ignorant about. I'll work to change that, whether or not you stick around. And I'll understand if you don't. But I hope—I hope that you do."

It was the hint of uncertainty that drew her in. That was when things between Nella and Miriam had shifted, from a delicious diversion to the main event.

Behind her, Miriam's table rises for a final round of hand-shaking and good nights. The men are in suits, the only other woman with hair like a dandelion clock. It's one of the many mysteries of scholars, how they take garden variety shabbiness and make it respectable. Miriam stands out, a hothouse bloom between them, immaculate in her emerald suit.

As the last of her colleagues zigzag from the room, Miriam saunters toward the bar.

"What are you doing so far south? You despise London."

Nella turns, drinking in the sight of her. "It has one or two sights I felt like seeing."

"You should have come over." Miriam leans against the bar, as close as she can get to Nella without touching. "Introduced yourself."

She shrugs. "That's what girlfriends do."

Miriam raises one slender eyebrow. "Isn't that what you are?"

"Not tonight."

Miriam is never slow on the uptake. Her smile widens, white teeth glinting. "Another of whatever this young lady's drinking," she says to the barman, "and a whisky for me. Double."

He doesn't hesitate, propelled into motion by those round vowels.

"Miriam Ashford." She holds out a hand.

"Nella Sorensen."

They shake, Miriam's grip firm and dry. Nella's heart hammers as Miriam claims the stool beside her, the material of her hand-tailored trousers skimming against Nella's bare skin.

"I don't usually do this." Nella toys with her straw. "Pick strangers up in bars, I mean."

"Then what brought you here tonight?"

Nella blushes, under the intensity of that gaze. "Just a feeling, I guess."

"And am I to believe," Miriam says with a smirk, "that you're some kind of ingenue?"

Nella looks up at Miriam from beneath her lashes. "What else would I be?"

Miriam leans in close. Her voice is low, breath hot against Nella's ear. "Oh, you are dangerous. Upstairs," she says. "Now."

Miriam hands her down from the stool, their drinks forgotten. The suit stares. Nella winks at him as they pass. Her legs are weak as they cross the hotel lobby, but Nella is steadied by Miriam's hand against the small of her back.

The elevator is waiting, empty. As they glide upward, the pit of Nella's stomach dips. Glancing at their reflection, she wonders: what might a stranger think they were to one another, her and Miriam? But the answer doesn't greatly concern Nella. Looking at Miriam, distinguished even with the tell-tale flush creeping above the neck of her shirt, Nella knows exactly what the older woman means to her. They sway to a stop, and the doors ease open.

Miriam gestures for Nella to step out into the carpeted hallway. Guides her to the room. As they step through the door, Nella is hit by a wave of the spicy cologne she favors.

She and Miriam fall on each other, door locking behind them. On Miriam's tongue Nella tastes the oaken burn of the whisky, and just a hint of smoke.

"I thought you were giving up."

"I thought you were an ingenue, come to my lair to be seduced."

Nella simply looks at her.

"Alright, alright," says Miriam. "I had one cigarillo, after dinner, not expecting to be caught. Though I am delighted with this surprise."

"I should punish you."

"Hmm. Perhaps the dominatrix, next time?"

Nella bats her lashes. "I wouldn't know how."

Miriam pulls her close, and as their lips meet again Nella forgets to be cross about the secret smoking, forgets everything except the feel of Miriam's arms snaking around her waist. Nella's world tilts as Miriam's hands whisper through the gossamer material of her dress.

The air is cool against Nella's back as Miriam unzips her.

The dress falls to the ground between them, hopelessly crushed as Nella stumbles back toward the bed, Miriam giving her no quarter.

"God, but you're beautiful."

Nella's blush is genuine, her cheeks warm. She goes to step out of her heels, but Miriam says, "No, keep them on."

"Kinky."

Miriam smiles, hooking her fingers around the sides of Nella's lace pants. She tugs until the scrap of material falls away. As they kiss, she unfastens Nella's bra in a single, expert motion. But when Nella goes to push Miriam's jacket from her shoulders, the older woman twists from her grasp.

"Oh, no. I have something else in mind. Sit down on the bed."

Nella does as she is bid, watching as Miriam brings the mirror over to stand at the foot of the bed. Then Miriam folds her jacket, drapes it over the back of the chair, steps out of her brogues, and sits them one beside the other. Nella's pulse quickens. Her heart pounds as Miriam crawls onto the bed, coming to sit behind her.

Miriam kisses a trail of fire down the slender column of her throat, nipping at the tender hollow until Nella gasps.

"Open your legs for me," she says. Miriam is never shy about what she wants.

Nella inches her thighs apart, exposing a sliver of pink.

"You're my ingenue," says Miriam. "And I'm going to teach you how to touch yourself just right, so that you think of me every time you come."

Miriam trails lazy circles around the dimpled skin of Nella's areola; her nipples stand, painfully taut even before Miriam begins to pluck at them.

"Wider," she says, pressing a kiss against Nella's shoulder.

She obeys. It's just as well Miriam sits firm behind her, because Nella feels weak from the want of it. She watches as Miriam's hand travels around her waist, up the smooth brown expanse of her thigh, and . . . away again.

Nella whimpers.

"Now, touch yourself for me. Run a finger along your lips." She caresses Nella's arm, feather soft, to demonstrate. "Like this."

Want pulses, a steady ache between Nella's thighs. She does not hesitate to ease it, skimming a finger against her sex. Miriam leans forward, avid.

"That's it," Miriam says. "Keep going."

Nella caresses herself until the velvet folds of her sex part, pink and glistening.

"Good." Miriam's hand massages the base of her neck; it's a firm, grinding pressure that Nella craves at the juncture of her thighs. In the mirror, Miriam's eyes twinkle with a glimmer of amusement; it's as if she can read Nella's thoughts. "Another finger. Gently."

At the crest of every stroke, Nella's fingers graze her clit. Oh, for the pressure of Miriam's touch. She gives a surreptitious rock of her hips—but of course Miriam feels it, sees it.

"Ah." Miriam catches her wrist, ignoring Nella's mewl of protest and lifts her hand, licking each finger clean. "You're getting ahead of yourself. Now, are you going to follow my instructions?"

"Yes, ma'am."

"All right." Miriam flicks at her nipple, and pleasure darts through Nella's body. "Now, back to it."

Nella watches with fascination as her mirror self, flushed and bright-eyed, slips two fingers inside her cunt and out again to trail that slickness around her clit. The wetness coats her thighs, soaks through the sheet beneath her pussy. She presses back against Miriam, rigid with the effort it takes to keep from tipping herself over the edge with a few even strokes.

"Good," says Miriam, cupping Nella's breast. She catches the nipple with the edge of her nail until Nella is moaning, all but sobbing, at the pleasure of it. "Very good."

Nella has never seen herself like this, plunging into the space between want and fulfilment. So wet that she's lost all inhibition. Is this how she looks through Miriam's eyes, when they fuck? It's audible, Nella's fingers dipping through her desire. She feels a shudder run through Miriam with every slick little pop.

"Now," she says, voice wavering, "I want you to stroke your clit until you can't stand it. That's when you come."

"But how will I know when I get there?" Nella bites her lip. "What if it never feels as good as you touching me?"

Now it's Miriam's self-control that shatters. Nella sees it in the darkening of her eyes, the spasm of her cheek. Before she can gloat, Miriam is on top of her, kissing Nella until she is breathless. She slides three fingers inside Nella, bent at the knuckle, thumb working at her clit until Nella is writhing against her, begging. "Oh, fuck—Miriam, please."

One of the heels falls away as Miriam rolls so that Nella sits astride her thigh, catching her clit at that angle Nella finds unbearable. This time, as Nella rocks her hips, Miriam whispers encouragement. "That's it. Just like that. Come for me."

Nella sways as waves of pleasure overtake her. She feels her cunt contract around Miriam's fingers, hears the throaty cry she dimly registers as her own.

But still Miriam frets at her clit, every touch acute. Her free hand supports Nella's back, and Miriam leans up to suckle at her breast. As her teeth catch the nipple, Nella trembles, tipping toward another orgasm.

Miriam's fingers drive in and out of Nella's sex, thumb

merciless at her clit. Until Nella shatters. She falls forward, forehead coming to rest against Miriam's, nudging those deft fingers away from her dripping core.

Nella's eyes close as Miriam presses a kiss against her temple. "Jesus, Miriam. I didn't know I could come that hard."

The tremor still runs through her leg, every nerve in Nella's body alight.

Miriam laughs, a throaty chuckle. "Not an ingenue anymore, then. But I'd wager you'll still think of me when you touch yourself."

Nella rocks against Miriam's thigh. "Who says I didn't already?"

"There she is. My debauched, darling Nellallitea."

"Just as well you like me." Nella shifts. "Because I've ruined your trousers."

"A small price to pay, for the privilege of ravaging such a nubile young thing. And it'll keep the dry cleaners from thinking I'm getting boring, with sixty on the horizon."

"Ha!"

"Want me to play the ingenue? Though I admit that might be a stretch."

Nella considers. "We could do late-in-life lesbian with first-time jitters. But no. I've got a better idea."

She kisses Miriam, tasting the brine of herself.

"Mm." Miriam pulls Nella's hair loose from the updo, trailing her fingertips along the shaved plane of Nella's scalp. "What's that, then?"

"You be Miriam, who's worn out after a day of talking about Tamara de Lempicka, drinking with her scholar colleagues, and fucking her stunningly beautiful girlfriend. I'll be Nella. And I think I'll strip you naked, hold you gently, and make love to you in this bed."

"That sounds . . . blissful. This Miriam has it pretty good."
Nella undoes the buttons of her shirt, planting a kiss after each
one, until Miriam cups her chin. "But are you sure? I did make
you work for it."

"Thanks to your handiwork, I'm feeling benevolent." Nella
smiles. "Besides, I've already given you wicked sex flush without
even touching you."

"What?" Miriam lurches upright, examining herself in the
mirror. "Oh, bloody hell."

Miriam's cheeks are flushed scarlet, the blush spreading
down her throat and across her chest. "God," she says, "that's
ridiculous."

"Ridiculously hot." Nella kneels behind her, nuzzling at
Miriam's neck as she pulls the shirt away. "Do you know how
much I love doing this to you?"

She unhooks Miriam's bra, flinging it from the bed, and cups
her breasts. Fuller than her own, if not quite as firm. A jolt runs
through Miriam, as Nella catches at her nipples. "It drives me
wild, seeing you go from being all debonair and in control to
desperately horny."

Miriam twists to kiss her. Slipping a hand between their
bodies, Nella unfastens the button of her trousers. As they fall
backward onto the mattress, Miriam wriggles free of the garment. Then she's flush against Nella, naked except for her pants.

Nella slides an arm beneath Miriam's bare shoulders, pulling
her close. As they kiss, Nella trails the fingers of her free hand
down Miriam's body—the swell of her breast, dip of her waist,
curve of her hip. She pulls Miriam's thigh to rest atop her own.

Nella cups Miriam's sex, feeling the heat and damp of her
through the thin cotton. Miriam swallows.

Nudging the elastic aside, Nella brushes her fingers through
the soft curls beneath. Their eyes lock. Nella dips one finger

inside Miriam's cunt. Then another. Miriam arches, but Nella covers her body with her own, fingers working urgently against that molten slickness.

She kisses the arc of Miriam's throat, pulse frantic against her lips. The mewling sound Miriam makes as Nella's thumb grazes her clit, again and again until she's frantic with pleasure, is divine. Miriam's desire trickles down her palm, coating the inside of Nella's wrist like a scent. She adds a third finger, Miriam's hips rising to meet her every thrust.

Nella relishes it, this ability to reduce such an articulate woman to a vocabulary of gasps and sighs. Miriam trembles against her, mouth working until—at last—she finds the words to beg. "Please. Nella, more . . . please—"

Nella knows exactly what it is that she needs. Peppering Miriam's forehead with kisses, Nella grinds a thumb against Miriam's clit until she's bucking hard. The orgasm rocks Miriam, core spasming round Nella's fingers. Then she is limp in Nella's arms, with a sleepy smile and tousled hair. Miriam, undone.

Nella strokes her back until Miriam's breathing evens, and though sleep drags at her eyelids, Nella stays awake. She savors the sight of Miriam, freshly fucked. No ingenue ever enjoyed such power. And no game matches it, the euphoria of knowing that she—Nella Sorenson, and no other—has so expertly unlocked the secrets of Miriam's body.

WELCOME
HOME

Quenby

"Aruba, Jamaica, oh I want to take ya
Bermuda, Bahama, come in me pretty mama"

Lex swung her hips to the rhythm of the song, feeling the plug shift inside her. A smile quirked her lips as she continued with the bastardized lyrics.

"Down on you, I will go
Not gotta take me to Kokomo . . . "

She trailed fingers along the curves of her body, feeling sensation dance across her skin. Her thumbs hooked into the waistband of sparkling booty shorts as she unconsciously ground her hips against the air, struggling against the temptation of temporary relief.

She held firm for a moment, then slipped fingers past her panties, feeling the slickness of her labia before pushing into her aching cunt. A moan filled the room as her practiced fingers stirred smoldering desire into burning *need*. For what felt

like the hundredth time since they started this game, Lex sent a
photo to her girlfriend.

Maya's phone buzzed as she sat in the taxi. She idly swiped
it open and grinned at the message. Lex's eyes were wide and
pleading, lip gripped between her teeth, fingers buried in her
shorts, and nipples all but poking through the "Pits and Perverts" top. Maya's cock twitched as she read the seven-character
caption. *Please?* She shook her head and smiled as she tapped
out a response.

Lex groaned as she read the reply. *Nice try pet! I'm literally
5 minutes away, I want you to be pathetic and needy when I get
home. You know that cunt belongs to me till the week is up so
Stop Touching Yourself!*

Meanie!!!!

Yes dear, that can happen when you date a sadist . . .

Lex rolled her eyes as she reluctantly stopped touching herself. *Love you . . . dick*

*You really are a slut for punishment aren't you? You know
I'm gonna make you pay for that . . .*

"Promise? <3

Lex set her phone aside and stood in the hall, squirming in
anticipation. She heard the taxi pull up outside, then the key rat-
tling in the lock. She pounced on Maya in a blur of excitement,
enveloping her girlfriend in a tight hug. "I missed youuuuuu."

Maya breathed in her scent for a moment, feeling Lex melt
against her as she kissed the top of her freshly shaved scalp.
Then she gently pushed her back, letting the subtle rhythms of
her domme voice settle into place. "Is this how you're supposed
to greet your mistress?"

Lex stepped back, blushing softly as the melodic commands
hotwired the subby parts of her brain. She dropped to her
knees, thighs spread provocatively wide and arms locked behind

her back. She waited in an agony of impatience, fighting the urge to rub her thighs together, while Maya studiously ignored her, bringing through her luggage and slowly hanging her coat. Finally her heels clicked to a halt, one boot sliding forward to softly press against Lex's crotch.

"I've been traveling for hours and you know trains make my back stiff, I should really rest." Her fingers slipped past Lex's lips and pressed against her tongue. "Is this seat taken?" Lex moaned in surprise around the violating fingers. Tears pricked her eyes as she began to fellate Maya's hand in a display of obscene eagerness. Maya laughed at Lex's disappointed groan as she withdrew her hand and wiped the clinging drool off on Lex's prickly scalp. Her expression melted into a soppy smile as Lex nuzzled affectionately, rubbing her face against Maya's fingers like a cat.

"Boots, kitten." Lex jumped at Maya's command, bowing down to kiss the toe of her knee-length boot before bringing it up against her chest. The ritual removal was carried out with reverential patience, laces untied then gently loosened eyelet by eyelet. Hands ran over the supple leather, feeling for dirt and scuff marks. Finally, one hand gripping the heel, she eased the boot from her lover's foot and put it in its place on the rack. Lex closed her eyes as Maya's thumb stroked across her sensitive scalp, losing herself for a moment in the touch she yearned for. With an effort, she managed to pull together enough composure to remove the other boot as well.

Maya leaned down, Lex's pliant lips yielding to her demanding kiss. Tongues danced together, stroking and teasing as they shared saliva. Lex whimpered softly when Maya pulled away, trying to follow the kiss and taste her lips for just a moment more. Maya gently pushed Lex back onto her knees, then leaned forward to whisper into her ear, "You know what I want, pet?

You know what I've been thinking of doing with you all week long?"

Lex let out a shaky breath at the sensation of warm air blown softly into her ear. Then she spoke in a voice husky with need. "What is it? I'll do anything you want, Mistress! Please, I need you!" Her hips writhed as she thought about all the ways she wanted to be used by her lover.

Maya smirked at the licentious display as she spoke. "I want . . . to sit down and enjoy a film with my girlfriend."

She laughed as Lex looked up at her like a kicked puppy, an expression of shock and betrayal on her face. "B-b-but . . . "

"Just because you spend all day dressed like a slut and dreaming about being used like a filthy little toy doesn't mean everyone does." Her tone shifted from teasing to commanding. "Now you're going to be a good girl and pick a film for us to watch. I decide when and how you get to be fucked, don't I?"

Lex whimpered in pathetic need, then pulled herself together enough to answer, "Yes, Mistress."

Maya stood up and strolled through to the kitchen. "Go pick a movie. I'll make us hot chocolate."

Pouting slightly, Lex got up and grabbed the remote from the sofa. Her lips pursed as she scrolled through some options, then broke into a smile as she saw the perfect choice. This would definitely break Maya's restraint and get her to stop being such a sadistic tease and *fuck her brains out already*. She took a couple of steadying breaths, aware that her inner monologue had been somewhat hijacked by her frustrated libido.

Maya walked back in, a conspicuous lack of hot chocolate in her hands. "I've thought of a game, darling. I'm going to get your vibrator, and shove it down those ridiculous sequined booty shorts you wanted to tempt me with. Every time you see something in the film that gives you a dirty thought you're going to turn it on and explain what turned you on this time. What do you think?"

"Is this a reward or a punishment?"

Maya tilted her head to the side and shrugged. "Both? I'm sure it won't be an issue though. Not unless you're a filthy little pervert who gets turned on by every little thing you see . . . . So what film did you pick?"

Lex looked down at the floor and mumbled, "*Charlie's Angels.*"

"The one with Kristen Stewart?"

"Yes."

"And all the other women who could destroy you with a single finger?"

"Maybe?"

Maya leaned back and let out a dirty chuckle. "Oh, you are so fucked, darling."

She leaned in to cut off her girlfriend's half-hearted protests with a kiss. Flustered, Lex leaned into the kiss. It started gently, soft lips caressing one another. Maya's hand cupped Lex's jaw and pulled her deeper into the kiss, tender affection morphing into fierce desire. Her tongue pushed deeper into Lex's mouth, sloppy and filthy and wonderfully obscene.

Maya opened her eyes as she moved her other hand into position. She smiled into the kiss as she pinched her girlfriend's nose shut. Lex's eyes opened in shock, as the kiss continued. Maya held her gaze, pupils large with sadistic lust as she drank in the heady cocktail of fear, desperation, and arousal. After what felt like an age she pulled away, letting Lex take undignified gasps of air as drool slipped from her lips.

Maya slipped a hand down Lex's shorts, giggling at the sodden panties she found there. "You're such a gross little slut!" She grinned as she anointed Lex's blazing cheeks with damp fingers.

She steered her slightly dazed sub to a place on the sofa, and pushed the head of a powerful wand vibrator into position inside her slutty shorts. She sat next to her and pressed play on the remote, as the opening credits rolled Lex turned to her and spoke in a hesitant voice. "Were you never planning to make hot chocolate, or have you had an ADHD moment?"

Maya froze for a split second and closed her eyes in mild exasperation at the slipup. Lex giggled slightly at the familiar expression, stopping abruptly as her domme arched an exquisite brow at her. Maya leaned in close. "It's. Your. Fault. I. Got. Distracted. You. Are. Too. Cute." Each word was punctuated by a slap to the face. Lex's cheeks stung and reverberated through her body and down to her cunt. Her stubbled scalp tingled with pleasure as Maya trailed delicate fingers over sensitized skin.

After a few minutes Maya came back from the kitchen, mugs in hand. She settled down on the sofa and took a sip of the rich cocoa as the familiar movie began to play. A grin twisted her face as Lex switched on the vibrator and began to grind against it.

Maya checked her watch; they were less than a minute in. "Come on, pet. Part of the game is that you tell me what you're perving on!"

"Unghh, uh, huh." Lex took a moment to breathe in and gather her thoughts. "Kristen Stewart looks really good in this scene and . . . uhhh . . . she was sucking the guy's fingers and that was hot too." She groaned in frustration as Maya leaned over and turned off the toy.

Maya shook her head. "We're like two minutes into the film and you're already this horny. Such a slut."

Lex blushed as she turned her attention back to the screen. Her eyes widened and she began grinding on the toy again. "I-I-I . . . . Fuck, I really want to get grappled and overpowered by all these women . . . "

Maya smiled to herself as she sat nursing her hot chocolate, listening to her girlfriend's desperate whimpers and moans. The vibrator stopped and started as Lex listed increasingly obscene fantasies and observations.

"The-the-the . . . *fuck*. The Bosley guy has soft daddy energy and I wanna soak his fucking beard. Oh, fuck, please, Maya . . . ."

"Your hot chocolate's getting cold, you should drink up." Frustration battled relief on Lex's flushed face as she reached down to pull the insistent toy from her booty shorts, but Maya reached over to grab her wrist. "Oh, no, we're still playing the game, pet." Lex looked at her with smoldering eyes; by now lust had burned away any residual shame, replacing it with feral need.

Trembling hands picked up her mug, a few drops rolling down the side as she raised it to her lips. She swallowed, barely tasting it as her focus on the film competed with clamoring demands by her cunt. "Oh, fuck . . . . is she wearing leather trousers?"

Maya turned on the vibrator, and leaned in to whisper in her ear, "Do you like that, slut? Are you picturing her pushing her knee up against your cunt? Your wetness smeared over the leather? Begging to worship her body the way you want to?" Lex threw her head back and let out a guttural moan as her hips bucked with unconstrained need. Cocoa slopped over the side of the mug and splattered on her top.

"Oh, look at that, you spilled the drink I made for you. Let's get you out of that top before you make more of a mess." Maya paused the film and turned off the vibrator, then peeled off the "Pits and Perverts" T-shirt. She watched her girlfriend's perky breasts bounce free, nipples dark and swollen. Maya straddled her lap and pinched the hard peaks as she leaned in. Lex savored the kiss and arched her back in response to the throbbing pain. Maya's cock brushed against her belly and she pushed back against it, feeling the familiar firmness and delicious promise.

Maya bit her lip and twisted harder, inhaling deeply as Lex whimpered for her. "Such a messy little slut. I'll have to teach you a lesson for wasting the drink I took the time to make."

Lex stood up once Maya had gotten off of her lap, then gasped as her sparkly sodden shorts were unceremoniously yanked down. "Yes Mistress, whatever you think I deserve!"

Maya moved behind her, her hand trailing over vulnerable flesh. Her thumb traced over Lex's agape lips, while her hands roughly groped her tits. At the same time, Maya explored her damp bush and slippery vulva. She maneuvered her into position and pushed her down over the arm of the sofa.

Maya knelt down behind her and slapped her hands onto Lex's cheeks, giggling at the moan it elicited. "Now what do we have here?" She reached out to grope and tease. "A ridiculously juicy cunt which is desperate to come. A cute little asshole stretched around a plug, just begging to get fucked." Her fingers hooked around the base of the plug, fucking back and forth. Lex let out a string of incomprehensible babbling as her ass fluttered around the motion. "Maybe I could just use this slutty little fuckhole and not let you come at all." Maya giggled at the pathetic noise Lex made in protest, then pushed the plug back in.

"First, though, I need to teach you a lesson!" Her hand smacked Lex, leaving a red print on one cheek then the other. Lex gasped in shock, then arched her back, presenting her taut buttocks. "Such. A. Fil-thy. Fuck-ing. Slut!" Each syllable was accompanied by a brutal smack. Lex squirmed and bucked, writhing with a heady mix of pleasure and pain. A savage grin twisted Maya's lips as she settled down to deliver a thorough beating.

Lex's perception of time melted away as she took countless blows. Maya varied the pace and power, mixing brutal slaps and punches with tender caresses. Lex felt her ass ache and burn as it was pulverized by her wonderful sadistic bastard of a soulmate, her cunt dripping on the sofa as she rode waves of exquisite agony. Finally she collapsed, sobbing in cathartic ecstasy.

Maya breathed heavily, her hands tingling with the price of sadism. She pulled her pale blue dress up over her head and threw it aside, leaving her naked besides her bra, sweat-slick hair sticking to her face. She wasted no time, pouring lube onto her thick cock, she pulled out Lex's plug and pushed her way in.

Lex groaned as Maya sank into her, inch after inch of cock stretching her ass. Maya watched her girlfriend's ass swallow her dick, gripping Lex's hips for leverage as her cock buried itself between Lex's bruised cheeks. Maya took a moment as she bottomed out, feeling the tight hole gripping her length. Then Maya began fucking her in earnest, driven by carnal hunger.

Lex moaned and drooled and dripped down her thighs. Words and thoughts were erased by the cock pounding into her with brutal, delicious force. She felt her worries and needs slip away as she surrendered herself to pure sensation, reduced to a collection of wet holes, she reveled in her nothingness.

Maya could feel her orgasm was close, but with a Herculean effort she stopped herself. She didn't want it yet, not like this. Pulling out, she dragged Lex with her as she went to sit on the chair, the time for teasing and subtle mind games well and truly over. She sat down, her fuck drunk sub staring hungrily at her cock.

Maya pulled her into position and pressed the vibrator into her hands. "Hold this against your cunt," she commanded, her voice guttural with lust. She hooked her arms under Lex's legs and around her back. She watched Lex's expression as she thrust back into her ass, feeling the rumbles of the vibe resonating through Lex's cunt and into her cock.

Lex's eyes were shut, drool filling the corners of her open mouth and a blissful smile spreading across her face as she was used as a mindless cocksleeve. Maya leaned forward and bit into her neck, then snarled into her ear, "Open your eyes. I want us to watch each other come." Lex's eyes snapped open at the command, eyes burning with indescribable need.

Lex ground her aching cunt against the vibrator, feeling the orgasm denied for so long build and build and build. Finally, as she fought to maintain eye contact as long as possible, her release took over. She screamed in overwhelming pleasure, legs jerked as sensation tore through her, ass clenching round Maya's cock. She squirted, fluid running down her cunt, past the vibrator still held in place, and onto the cock still fucking into her.

Maya let out a primal snarl, thrusting up one, two, three more times before coming deep inside her lover. Her breath stuttered, nails digging into Lex's back as she staked her obscene claim.

They stayed like that for a perfect moment, reveling in the shared sensations. Staring deep into one another's eyes, great waves of raw emotion rolled back and forth between them, bound by lust and love and vulnerability. Then Lex leaned forward and planted a kiss on Maya's lips. "Welcome home, Maya. I really missed you."

Maya giggled. "I missed you, too. But if that's the reception I get when I return, maybe I should go away more often?"

Lex stuck her tongue out. "So you're saying I shouldn't make a habit of this. Well, if you're sure . . . "

The two of them devolved into helpless giggles as they

exchanged a volley of kisses along one another's faces and
neck. Then Maya pulled her forward into a proper snog,
tender and intense all at once. They pulled apart again and, a
little breathless, Maya held her lover in a tight hug. "I love you,
Lex, so much." And for a moment, that's all that mattered.

DIRNDL
DARLING

Noel Stevens

"I look ridiculous in this."

"You look like a tall stein of *weizen* that I want to drink up, *liebling*," Marc said, smoothing his hands over my shoulders as I looked at my reflection in our hotel room mirror.

I shot my husband a look of annoyance in the mirror, but then softened, remembering why we were here.

After his health scare last year, Marc announced that we would be filing notices of unavailability on all our pending court cases at work, leaving the kids with his mother, and embarking on his bucket list.

Item one on Marc's bucket list: Oktoberfest.

Not the dingy party at our local craft brewery, but the real-deal, two-week-long Oktoberfest, in Munich. He wanted to go all out.

Hence, why I was dressed like a ridiculous Strawberry Shortcake—with tits. No Party City polyester outfits for Marc's bucket list. Oh, no.

* * *

The day before, he had dragged me to an entire department store dedicated to traditional German folk costumes. He headed to the men's section, leaving me alone with an older German woman, who was nice enough, but spoke no English. And I spoke no German, since I had been relying on Marc to guide us through the trip on his frantic two months of Duolingo lessons. She ushered me into the dressing rooms and handed me a frilly white blouse. Well, half of a blouse, if I was being generous. It was more of a bra with sleeves.

"Where's the rest of it?" I asked.

The woman pointed to her own breasts before pushing another hanger into my hands. *"Pinkfarben."*

Once alone in the dressing room, I undressed and then tackled trying to squeeze into the blouse contraption. As I expected, it barely covered my whole breasts. Shaking my head, I slid into the dirndl that she had shoved into my hands. Apart from the garish pink color I would have never picked for myself, I supposed it wasn't too bad. It was basically a fit-and-flare A-line that fell to my knees and nestled into the blouse. I pulled back the curtain.

"Pinkfarben!" the woman exclaimed, clapping her hands excitedly. She pulled a ribbon from her pocket and quickly began lacing it through the hooks on the front of my dirndl.

"That's a little tight," I said on a sharp inhale.

"Pinkfarben," she muttered, with a final tug on the ribbon. I looked down at my breasts, which were at a height they had never before achieved and were spilling over the top of the blouse. It was nearly obscene. The woman tied an apron—an apron!—around my waist.

"You look beautiful."

I tore my eyes away from my breasts and looked up. Marc

leaned against the wall, completely decked out in brown leather lederhosen that went only to his knees, knit stockings that hugged his calves, and a red-and-white checkered shirt. He should have looked ridiculous, but the sight of him caused my breath to catch in my chest. Maybe it was the way his shirt sleeves were rolled up, revealing his strong forearms. Maybe it was how at ease and happy Marc seemed. Or maybe it was the ribbon and hooks squeezing my internal organs together.

"I feel like we're playing dress-up," I said, once I regained my composure.

"Good. You deserve to play, *liebling*," he smirked at me. I could feel a flush spread across my face and breasts.

I pulled the curtain of the dressing room shut, closing myself inside.

It was ten in the morning on a Tuesday, and I was walking down a carnival midway in a puffy blouse and apron, with my tits hiked up near my chin. Marc, meanwhile, was clearly in his element. This was the giddiest I had seen him in a very, very long time. He was nearly skipping as we walked through the gates and heard the first deep notes and cymbal hits of *"Ein Prosit"* float over us from a distant beer tent. His fingers kept brushing against mine, intermittently interlacing with mine to pull me toward each carnival game or ride that caught his interest.

"Want to go on the Tunnel of Love, *liebling*?"

I rolled my eyes. "Let's just try to get a seat at a beer tent before it gets too crowded."

Marc's eyes lit up, a corner of his mouth raised in a smirk. "I love your priorities."

"I just don't want to get stuck standing all day," I muttered, though Marc didn't hear me. He was on a mission. He guided us toward a "beer tent," though I wondered if something was getting lost in translation, because these giant buildings didn't look like any sort of tent I had ever seen. Breweries had their own tents, and they seemed determined to outdo each other; one tent entrance was guarded over by a giant animatronic lion growling as he chugged a stein of beer.

Once inside a tent, it was even more elaborate than the outside. The two-story wooden frame was strewn with banners and flags. The tent could easily fit a few thousand people, but as it was still fairly early on a Tuesday morning, the tables were not too crowded yet. The brass polka band was just beginning to set up in the center gazebo stage.

We grabbed a seat at an empty table on the first floor, and a waitress clad in similar attire as me dropped two menus off. I quickly scanned the front and back of the menu as I took my phone out of my dirndl pocket.

"What are you thinking?" Marc asked, his eyebrows wagging. "Start slow by splitting a liter, or should we each get our own?"

"I'm looking for the wifi password. I don't see it printed on the menu." I craned my neck, looking for the waitress. Maybe she would know it.

Marc laughed. "I don't think the tents have wifi. Why do you need it, anyway?"

"Because I can't get any bars in here, despite that expensive international data plan we bought."

"Yeah, but you don't need your phone right now. Let's just enjoy ourselves." He slid his hand across the table and placed it on top of mine. I shook his hand off and grabbed my phone, lifting it higher to see if I could pick up any bars.

"I need to check my work email."

"It's the middle of the night at home." Marc sighed.

"Yes, but as we were leaving the hotel, I saw an email come in from a client."

He peeked his face around my phone, locking his eyes with mine. "And your paralegal is more than capable of handling that in the morning. You're on vacation. The office can survive without you for this one week."

I pursed my lips. "It looked like it could be important. They might be trying to avoid a warrant."

Marc sank back into his chair with a sigh and looked around the tent. "I guess you can go to the upper floor and see if you can get a better signal from there."

"Good idea." I hopped up from my seat. "I'll just respond to a few emails, and then I'll be right back. You won't even miss me."

Marc grumbled something I couldn't quite make out while I headed toward the staircase. Luckily, the upper floor was deserted, so no one would see my embarrassingly desperate attempts to get a signal. I knew I *should* unplug on vacation, especially since this trip meant so much to Marc. But I didn't necessarily know *how*. My work was important, and often all-consuming. I didn't know how to just *be*—especially around Marc, ever since he was sick last year. It had been a really scary time, and a busy time, as we added his medical appointments to our already too long to-do lists of balancing kids and our jobs. This trip was our first real time alone together since, and I didn't really know what to do with myself, alone, with my husband.

I headed to the back corner of the tent and propped my elbows up against the balcony that looked out onto the main floor. My eyes swept over the rows of tables looking for Marc but I didn't spot him, so I soon returned my attention to my phone. My signal didn't seem any better on this floor, but I kept trying, turning my data on and off.

Suddenly, I felt a heavy weight behind me, leaning into and pinning me against the balcony banister.

My heart leapt from my chest, and I let out a scream, but it was easily drowned out by the tuba in the band and the other sounds of revelry below. I began to thrash against the person—until I noticed the familiar wedding ring on his left hand as it reached for my phone.

"Marc!" I yelled. "You scared the shit out of me!"

His right hand soothed my back as he took my phone and pocketed it. My pounding heart began to calm down.

"Sorry, I didn't mean to scare you. You just looked too good standing here. And I missed you."

"I was only gone for a second."

"No. I've missed you. I've missed us," he whispered against my neck, planting a soft kiss against my neck.

A shiver shot down my spine, and I was flooded with feelings I hadn't experienced in some time. Between Marc's health scare, the kids, and work, it had been a while since we'd been even this intimate with each other.

His hands moved from my back to the balcony railing, planting them on either side of me as he deepened the kiss on my neck. Marc knew that my neck was especially sensitive, that any kiss, lick, or bite sent an immediate volt straight to my clit. As his teeth grazed against my sensitive skin, I let out a small moan. A warmth spread underneath my dirndl and my knees shook the tiniest bit, causing Marc to tighten his hold on me against the banister.

"Marc," I whispered breathily. "We're in public."

"We're the only ones up here. But tell me when you want me to stop," he murmured against my throat, as he slid his hands from the banister up the laces of my dirndl and teased the front of my blouse. His fingers circled my nipples through the fabric. I let out a strangled moan as my nipples hardened through the fabric and my clit began to throb. "Oh, and no one can hear you up here. Not over the polka band."

I looked down at the floor below. The waitstaff seemed too busy with dishing out liters of beer and the revelers seemed too distracted by those beers to look up and check for an old married couple making out upstairs. But if anyone did look up, they would definitely be able to see my husband sucking at my neck and groping at my breast like we're a couple of horny teenagers. Maybe that wasn't extremely unusual drunken Oktoberfest behavior that would attract much attention, but it was certainly unusual for us. And Marc was right; the *oom-pah-pah* of the band would certainly drown out any happy little sounds I might make.

Except that I let out a deep, guttural groan as Marc slid his hands into my blouse, cupping the bare skin of my breasts. He squeezed and rolled my nipples between his fingers. Hot liquid pooled between my thighs as I let out another moan. To anyone looking up, this wouldn't look like some amorous PDA. This was obscene.

"Marc," I panted. "We can't—"

"Tell me to stop," he said, nipping at my jaw.

I should have told him to stop. I willed myself to tell him to stop. But I didn't want him to. It felt so good to be touched like this again. To feel his possessive hold on my body. To feel breathless and wild, despite all the potential onlookers below who might catch us. Maybe especially because someone might catch us.

So instead, I dropped my head and shoulders forward and pushed my ass up against his form as I let out another groan. Marc responded by flipping down my blouse, fully exposing my breasts. I may have thought my breasts were spilling out of my blouse before, but now I could see my hardened nipples as Marc teased them. The sight of Marc's hands on my bare breasts, overlooking the beer hall below, made me buck my hips back against him. I was searching for any sort of friction, any sort of relief against his body.

"You're incorrigible," I grunted. "But don't stop."

His right hand left my breast and slid down my dirndl, across my stomach, hip, and thigh. When he reached the hem, he bunched the fabric up in his hand and dragged it slowly up my thigh. I gasped as his hand slipped beneath the fabric of my skirt. His hand clutched at my bare thigh and slowly made its way over to my panties. My clit throbbed, aching for his touch, but he seemed intent on teasing me, instead fiddling with the lace on my panties. I rocked my hips back, urging him to give me some of the relief that I craved.

"Marc," I groaned.

"Is there something you want, *liebling*?"

"Yes," I grunted, grinding against him. Despite his leather lederhosen, I could make out the shape of his erection.

"Tell me," he said, his fingers infinitesimally inching toward the edge of my panties.

"I want . . . " I trailed off, trying to get the courage to speak the words out loud in public.

"Yes? What do you want?" His fingers moved away from the edge of my panties, but traveled downward. He dragged the pads of his fingers over my panties from my labia to my clit. I inhaled sharply as the slightest hint of relief was replaced with an even greater need. At the sound of my inhale, he paused for a moment on top of my clit, before dragging his fingers back over my labia. They were swollen, protruding out of the edges of my panties, which were completely soaked. He lightly pushed the heel of his palm against my clit. I shuddered against his frame, but Marc stilled his hand.

"Tell me what you want," he said firmly.

"I want . . . " I gulped, summoning the courage. "I want . . . your fingers."

"Fingers? Naughty *liebling*," he said as he moved my

drenched panties to the side and plunged two of his fingers into my cunt. I exhaled as he curled his fingers against my walls and his thumb found my clit. My walls clenched around his fingers and he continued to stroke, but I wanted more. I moved against his hand, urging him on.

"Is this what you want? Or do you want more?"

Unable to speak, I whimpered, nodding my head. His fingers picked up speed and he slid a third finger into me. My knees trembled, and I leaned into the banister for support. The shift in position sunk his fingers deeper in, hitting a delicious new spot within me. My breasts bounced against the railing as I rode Marc's slick fingers, seeking out the release that I could feel the early beginnings of. But this new position also pushed my ass firmly against Marc's now very prominent erection. Marc, who had been so solid and stoic throughout our entire escapade, let out a small groan as my ass rubbed up against him. I slightly backed off chasing my release, and focused on stroking Marc's erection with my ass. He groaned again.

"Marc?" I asked breathily.

He cleared his throat. "Yeah?"

"What do you want?"

He leaned forward, nibbling at my neck. "I want you to come on my fingers."

I ran my ass over the length of his erection again. "Is there anything else you want?"

He pulled me even closer against his chest as his fingers picked up speed and his tongue lavished my neck. "Yes," he breathed against my throat.

I moaned as his hot breath sent another tingle to my clit. I could burst on his fingers at any moment, but I took a deep breath, trying to hold off. I couldn't believe what I was proposing, but I knew I wanted it.

"Is it complicated to get you out of your outfit, or . . . ?"

"That's actually the brilliance of the lederhosen's design," Marc said, then chuckled. His fingers withdrew from me, leaving an even stronger, pounding need in their wake. His other hand dropped from my waist. I looked over my shoulder and watched as his hands went to the buttons at the top of his lederhosen. I squeezed my thighs together, hoping to ease the throbbing of my clit as I watched him undo one button, and then another, and brought the flap down.

Hot liquid pooled between my thighs and began to drip down. "You're not wearing any boxers!"

His bare cock stared straight ahead at me. I had seen his penis a thousand times before, but I don't know if I have ever seen it this thick and erect. A small bead of precome glistened at its head. I licked my lips and exhaled. It had been a long time since it had had this much of an effect on me.

Marc just smiled, a devilish glint in his eye as he shrugged one shoulder. "They told me at the store this was the traditional way to wear them."

"Well, thanks to the store, I guess."

"Yeah, I've been silently thanking them ever since I realized you were braless," he said with a smirk, sending a tingle directly to my still-hardened nipples.

He leaned back into me, placing his hands on either side of my waist and stabilizing us against the railing. I looked out onto the floor below, seeing if anyone was noticing that I was about to fuck my husband on this balcony. In that moment, I didn't necessarily care who saw us.

Marc's hands gathered up the back of my skirt and brought it over to cover his exposed penis. His hard dick slapped against my ass, before traveling down to rest beneath my soaking, throbbing cunt. I whimpered as the head gently rubbed against my opening, my wet panties still pushed to the side.

"Are you sure this is what you want, *liebling?*" he asked, nibbling at my neck.

I responded by sinking my ass further against him, rubbing myself along the length of his dick. He grabbed my hips and pulled me closer to him. His hand left its grip on my hip as he position his penis outside my entrance. My cunt trembled at the light contact. I groaned, leaning my breasts further into the banister, as my pussy took in an inch of his hardness. I needed more, but Marc was still and unmoving. I knew what he wanted. Clenching my inner walls, I eased myself back slowly, taking all of him in, inch by inch. Marc exhaled behind me. I felt deliciously full, but needed so much more. I pushed back just a little further, urging him on.

His hands gripped onto my hips, and he slowly slid back until he was nearly out of me. I tightened my grip on the banister and whimpered, before he slammed fully back into me, hitting the delicious spot his fingers had found earlier. Over and over again. Using my grip on the railing, I met his thrusts. I was already panting as Marc's right hand trailed around my hip to my clit. His finger whisked up some of my wetness and brought it to my clit, circling around it. I groaned at the intensity, dropping my head against my arms on the banister to try to keep my bearings. Marc quickened the pace of his thrusts, and I let out loud yips as each impact brought me closer and closer to orgasm.

I suddenly realized if the band went on break, the fest-goers and waitstaff would be privy to some pretty unseemly sounds escaping from my mouth, a thought which somehow managed to only spur me on. I moved my hips faster against Marc, bringing myself further up the wave toward completion. We heaved our bodies against each other, as if powered by all of the anxiety and worry that we had coiled within ourselves over the past year. I was throwing myself on him, opening to him in a way I should have this entire year, instead of closing myself off. He was my husband. I loved him. I had been scared to lose him, and didn't know what to do with those feelings. But this? This closeness. This vulnerability. This felt right. This is what I had needed.

Finally, the relief broke over me, and I let out a scream, collapsing onto the railing as I let the wave wash over me, my inner walls fluttering around him.

He grabbed me around the waist and chest, holding me tight against him during his last powerful thrusts as he finished. I panted for breath, reveling in the feeling of security and contentment in his tight embrace. I let out a relieved laugh as I rested against him, not believing we had actually gotten away with this, just as I heard a round of applause.

I peeked over the banister and saw the band waving to the crowd as they set down their instruments. As the band took their break, there went much of our cover. Marc could sense it as well. I slid off of him, straightening my dirndl. Marc tucked himself back into his lederhosen and quickly buttoned up.

"I have a confession." He leaned forward, whispering in my ear. "That was my actual bucket list item."

I turned and placed a gentle kiss on his lips. "Well, I could use about a liter of beer. And one of those giant pretzels."

He smacked my ass as we headed for the staircase, before taking my hand in his. "What, too early in the morning for sausage, *liebling*?"

THE LAST NIGHT

Katrina Jackson

Some relationships end with a bang, some with a whimper, but Kara's first serious relationship died a slow, expected death. For years after it was over, she always marked the official end date as the day her boyfriend Christian married their girlfriend Qiana, but in reality, that relationship had been dying ever since the day he proposed. It wasn't a surprise. They'd made the decision together. It made so much sense at the time, but heartbreak has no logic.

"This is beautiful!" Qiana squealed, breezing into the room.

Kara hadn't heard the hotel door open, and the melodic sound of Qiana's voice shocked her, making her heart thud against her chest. She didn't turn around immediately. Instead, she scanned the room up and down, left and right, taking her hard work in, trying to see it through Qiana's eyes. It was the night before the wedding, and conflicting emotions aside, Kara wanted the bride to feel special. All the magazines she'd read said easing the bride's worries was an important part of a bridesmaid's duties.

Sadly, none of the articles had suggestions for how a spare girl-friend could manage her feelings in the face of rejection, but she'd soldiered on, nonetheless. In the end, event planning had been the perfect distraction from the mix of happiness and sadness warring inside her soul as the wedding day approached faster than she could handle.

"You like it?" Kara asked, her voice breaking right along with her heart.

Qiana rolled her eyes. "Girl, yes. This is beautiful. But you really didn't need to do all this. You've already done so much."

That last part was very true. Kara had helped Qiana and Christian plan their wedding, while small pieces of her heart chipped away. She tagged along like a third wheel while they visited possible venues, tasted wedding cake, and worked on the seating chart. She was right there by Qiana's side as the bride tried on nearly a hundred wedding dresses before she found the one. She felt Qiana's excitement as her own and pretended the tears pooling in her eyes were from happiness rather than despair. And then they'd locked the changing room door behind them. Kara pushed yards of tulle and lace up Qiana's legs and kissed her way up her thighs. Kara had punctuated the triumphant moment by using her mouth on Qiana, sucking and licking and tasting her girlfriend until the other woman's shaking thighs wrapped around her head. Qiana muffled the sound of her swallowed moans with her hands. Kara made Qiana come with her mouth and fingers, trying to make the rest of the dress shop and the world disappear in their ecstasy.

In hindsight, Kara realized that their risky public sex had been her feeble attempt to reassert herself in their relationship. She'd wanted Qiana to come on her tongue to remind them both that no one ate her out the way Kara did. Not even Christian. It was childish and petty. But in her defense, they *were* only

twenty-six and denial could be so addictive right up until it was
time to face the truth.

So, yes, Kara did need to do all this because tonight she was
saying goodbye.

"Where did you even find the time?" Qiana gasped, setting
her suitcase down and gently placing the extra-large garment
bag with her wedding dress inside over the back of the couch.

Kara shrugged, unsure how to answer that question, eventually deciding it was best to avoid it completely. "I wanted you to
be happy," was all she could muster. Her voice was tight, full of
barely contained emotion. She'd spent months worrying if she
sounded happy or sad or annoyed, so often modulating her tone
to hide her true feelings, and now she was spent. This was as
close to normal as she could manage, but Qiana and Christian
didn't know the truth, and tonight, that was all that mattered.

They locked eyes across the sitting room, Qiana's already
brimming with tears. There was a lump in Kara's throat.

Kara remembered the day they met so clearly. They were
sophomores in college, and the three of them had rented a room
apiece in a house a few blocks from campus that looked better online than in person. Kara had been close to tears walking from one dark room to another, testing the strength of the
bars on the windows, trying to ignore the constant dripping
of the bathroom faucet, wondering why the house smelled like
burned cooking oil, hoping she could get her deposit back. But
then Qiana had walked through the front door, big white smile
on her face, flushed brown skin, perfectly applied inky black
winged eyeliner, and an adorable laugh, and Kara had thought
there was no way this apartment could be as bad as it seemed.
By the time Christian arrived, she'd been half in love with Qiana
but still had room in her heart for him.

That was six years ago, and strangely enough, she still felt as

in love with Qiana as that first day. "Are you happy?" Her voice
was a pathetic whisper now.

"Yes, babe." Qiana's whisper, suffused with love, was anything but pathetic. She rushed across the room and wrapped her
arms around Kara's shoulders, a few tears finally falling over
her cheeks.

When their mouths touched, Kara could taste the salty happiness of Qiana's lips, the spearmint of her tongue. She wondered if Qiana could taste the shot of vodka she'd downed after
pushing half a dozen explicit cupcakes for the bride and groom
into the refrigerator. But she wouldn't ask because she was a
coward. Kara wouldn't have to wait years to figure that out
about herself. She'd been scared to death of losing the two people she loved most in the world, and what had she done to stop
it? Nothing.

Thankfully, timidity had no taste.

"This is dope!" Once again, Kara hadn't heard the door
open, but Christian's voice filled the room, sliding into all the
gaps between them.

In college, he'd been a second-string tight end on the football
team. He played just well enough to keep his scholarship but not
so good that he risked being upgraded to the first line or serious injury. He spent more time in the Public Relations Society
than at the student-athlete mixers because he had a plan for
his life—for their life—and football was only a stepping stone,
never the destination. Kara had always assumed that marriage
wasn't part of their plan either, but she'd been wrong.

Kara looked over Qiana's shoulder at Christian. She wanted
to memorize the look of shock and innocent glee on his face,
the way his forehead wrinkled with his smile, the smell of his
cologne filling the room and tickling her nose, and the feeling
of Qiana's breasts pressing into hers. But she'd never be able to

remember this moment without wondering if he already knew that this was the end.

"Kara did all this, and we didn't even know," she said, smiling in Christian's direction before turning back to Kara. She brushed the pads of her thumbs over the sharp line of Kara's jaw. "She surprised us." Her voice was a breathy sigh full of wonder, and her eyes were bright with happiness. Kara would remember Qiana like this always, even years later, late at night in the privacy of her home, where she could touch herself and cry and come without judgment, but with lots of shame and far too much grief to hold inside her.

"I wanted you to love it," Kara admitted to Qiana.

"I do," the other woman said, soft but serious.

"What about me?" Christian asked. He'd come closer while Kara and Qiana had gotten lost in one another. He wrapped his body around Qiana's back, his hands landing big and strong on Kara's hips, pulling her closer against Qiana. Against them.

Kara sighed in his hold, closing her eyes at the feeling of safety she always felt when they held each other like this, so many arms and hands and fingers and soft kisses here in their own world.

"Didn't you want me to love it, too?" Christian asked.

Qiana rolled her eyes. "You think cardboard boxes are furniture," she said. "Kara could have decorated this place with a platter of wings and Patrón and you'd have been happy."

"Was that an option?" Christian asked excitedly.

Kara laughed despite the gaping pit of despair in her chest. It was hard to discern the violent shifts in her mood. Sinking depression, soaring love, a premature grief running through it all.

And then there was the lust.

Christian pulled Kara closer and moved his hands to her ass, kneading the soft flesh roughly. Kara's eyes shot open as her peal of laughter died out in a shocked gasp that Qiana caught in her hungry mouth. She lapped up that sound and every moan Christian pulled from Kara with his insistent fingers.

"I'm serious," Christian insisted, his mouth close enough to theirs that he could join this kiss if he wanted. If they wanted.

They did.

According to Qiana, there was an art to kissing anyone, but especially kissing more than one person at a time. When they'd first started messing around, she'd taken it upon herself to teach Kara and Christian everything she knew about the joy of three-somes—her favorite kind of sex. She considered every orgasm they managed to wring from one another a sign of her expert instruction. She had always been a great teacher, but she said Christian was the kind of student who would make anyone tear their hair out.

Even though Kara and Qiana had turned toward him, making room for his tongue in the cavern of their mouths, he smiled and pressed his lips to the corner of Kara's eye, softly, letting that touch linger. This was something Qiana hadn't taught him, something Christian had understood better than any of them— how to make every touch, every word, every slam of his hips move beyond the physical into a soul-searing memory that was damn hard to forget.

For years, Kara would wake up in the middle of the night, the ghostly press of Christian's dick slipping inside of her, shocking her brain and her heart awake. She'd feel a dull throb in her pussy and recognize it as some memory reasserting itself from a sexual encounter she couldn't quite recall but also couldn't seem to forget. But these kisses she remembered always.

He placed soft butterfly pecks down her left cheek, moving slowly toward her mouth. Kara and Qiana's tongues tangled together, sensuously waiting for him to complete them, while their hands grazed one another's waists and chests, brushing Christian's arms and his jaw, cupping the back of his head when his mouth was so close, finally pulling his tongue inside their mouths. This kiss was hungry, possessive, and for Kara, bittersweet. She kissed them as if her heart hadn't been ground to dust by rejection. That was the least she could do.

Christian could feel Kara pulling away.

Their relationship was a delicate balance that had worked right from the beginning. Qiana was bright and bubbly, Christian was big and soft, and Kara was warm and too serious. Just two worked fine, but when they were all three together, Qiana said they were the best melody.

She'd been high off a few orgasms and an edible sugar cookie at the time, but it had made perfect sense, and so it stuck.

But they only harmonized when they gave their all to the relationship, and Christian had felt the moment Kara started to drift away. Six months of watching the mask she usually only wore at school or work invade their home. Six months of knowing they were losing Kara and not being able to fix whatever they'd broken.

But he never stopped trying to convince her to stay.

"If there ain't no wings, then let's go to bed," he mumbled against their mouths.

He loved the way Kara and Qiana's laughter blended together but always remained distinct to his ears. How they held onto one another and him as they walked from the sitting room into the bedroom. The way Qiana gasped when she saw the rose petals on the bed and their sex toys lined up on the dresser. The way Kara could always make him laugh, even when everything else hurt. The shy but proud smile on her face at their reactions. His own happiness as they leaned against his body.

"Seriously, Kara, you didn't need to do this!" Qiana said, moving to the bed, reaching for the rose petals nervously as if she thought they would disappear when she touched them.

Christian felt Kara shrug. He reached down and grabbed her hand. She gripped his hand as tight as she could and pressed herself against his side. The desperation he felt in those movements broke his heart.

"Get naked," he said, his voice deeper than normal, full of emotion, lust, need, sadness.

Kara shivered against him, gripping his forearm with her other hand, holding him so tight her nails threatened to break the skin. Qiana turned around and began to undress, a triumphant smile on her face.

Christian listened to Kara's breath hitch and bent over to kiss her forehead, closing his eyes, breathing her in. He could discern how naked Qiana was based on Kara's excitement. He'd always loved seeing them through one another's eyes.

"G-get on the bed," Kara stuttered.

Christian smiled against Kara's skin and whispered to her.

"Spread your legs," Kara said, her voice strengthening now that she could give voice to his desires, which always mirrored her own.

Qiana's giggles mixed with the sound of her feet moving over the bedspread.

"What next?" Kara whispered to him. She sounded almost normal now. Hungry. Excited. Ready.

Christian felt a sudden pang of determination that this might work. Things were always easiest in moments like this, when they could be naked with one another in all the ways that counted. It was when the world outside infringed on this sacred space that everything got all messed up. But they'd decided on the marriage together—all three of them—and he couldn't understand how it had all gone so wrong.

When Qiana lost her job, they all knew she needed health insurance before her old policy lapsed. She had sickle cell anemia. Kara was still in graduate school, and her student health insurance barely covered her own needs; meanwhile, Christian had a good entry-level position at one of the best entertainment public relations firms in the city. The decision was a no-brainer. Of course, he would marry Qiana, but nothing about their relationship had to change.

Nothing was supposed to change. But it did.

"Tell her to touch herself," he said, knowing how much they loved that. Right from the beginning. The first time a drinking game went too far, and they found themselves in their living room in that shitty first apartment, butt naked, touching themselves together weeks before they ever touched each other.

"Play with your pussy," Kara groaned, moving closer to Christian.

He kissed his way down the bridge of her nose and lifted his free hand to tilt her head back. His mouth hovered above hers, tasting her breath and a shot of vodka. He wondered if she was just pregaming or if she'd needed that drink to steel her nerves. He hoped it wasn't the latter.

"Get naked," he told her, and his lips brushed hers as he spoke.

She smiled against his mouth and then lifted up on the balls of her feet to kiss him hard.

Christian smiled and lifted her into his arms. He tasted Qiana on her tongue during this kiss. She wrapped her legs around his waist, swallowing her laughter when her pussy rubbed against his dick.

He walked them to the bed, and they fell across it.

Qiana shrieked and jumped out of the way, laughing excitedly. Christian ground his hips into Kara, and they shifted up the bed, pulling the comforter and sheets with them. It was messy, uncoordinated, and full of love.

He groaned in relief as they finally hit their groove.

Qiana's nails scraped his back as she pulled his T-shirt up. He lifted from Kara's body, letting her mouth go reluctantly, helping Qiana strip his shirt off. She let him go, and he stood, his fingers fumbling with his belt as he kicked off his shoes.

Meanwhile, Qiana climbed over Kara, her pretty fingernails pushing Kara's leggings and underwear down her legs.

"Help me," she whined, looking up at Christian with a playful smile.

Christian rolled his eyes, pushed his jeans down his legs, and bent down to pull Kara's legs free.

Qiana pulled Kara's thighs open. His eyes went to her pussy, wet, the flash of pink between dark brown lips, Kara's moan, Qiana's fingers smoothing down the cleft as she pulled Kara's lips open for his gaze. "Help me," she said again, nothing playful about her voice this time.

Christian fell to his knees at the foot of the bed and pulled Qiana's mouth to his. They kissed each other quick and hard while Kara squirmed beneath Qiana's body. As soon as he pulled back, Qiana's free hand was at the crown of his head, guiding his mouth to Kara's other lips.

"Fuck," Qiana hissed, letting him know that Kara's mouth was occupied as well.

He smoothed his hands over Kara's inner thighs, already trembling in excitement. His dick was achingly hard now, leaking precome from the tip, but he could wait. They had all night. He only hoped they had the rest of their lives. He tried to bury the small lightning bolt of fear that they didn't, that this was it. But he channeled that small shock by licking Kara's pussy— and Qiana's fingers—with a kind of possessive hard swipe they all knew too well. He tasted Kara from opening to clit and back again, getting lost in every part of her. He suckled at her clit until Qiana nudged his head to the side so she could help.

They both smiled when Kara screamed out her first orgasm of the night from Qiana's lips around her clit and his tongue and fingers in her opening. And then Qiana settled her own pussy back onto Kara's mouth, muffling those moans as they kept eating her out until she was shaking, on the verge of another release.

This had to be enough to keep her, Christian thought.

It had to be.

Christian's warm breath ghosted up Kara's spine, and it made her shiver.

"It's okay, baby," Qiana whispered against Kara's mouth. Her hand gripped Kara's throat in a loose hold, gentle as ever. Her eyes were deep pools of warmth. Love. So many emotions Kara wanted to hide from, but she couldn't look away. "Stay here with me. This is where we belong."

Kara wanted to cry at Qiana's words, her touch, the taste of her pussy still lingering on her tongue, and then Christian's dick pushing into her pussy from the back, pressing her body forward into Qiana's waiting mouth.

"It's just us, baby," Qiana whispered as Kara's hips rocked back into Christian.

And then he surged forward, ripping a scream from Kara's throat.

Qiana smiled and whispered again. "Just us."

"Just us," Christian panted, fucking into Kara. "Stay with us."

"Please," Kara begged.

Qiana kissed Kara again, smiling against her mouth. "Say it, Kara."

Christian's hips started moving faster, their skin slapping together, his grunts mixing with her moans.

"Say you'll stay, baby," Qiana begged. "Say it, and I'll crawl under you and suck your clit."

Kara came with a sharp cry. "I love you," she groaned. "It's just us."

Qiana smiled and kissed Kara's chin. "We love you too, baby," she said and proved it by crawling onto her back and shimmying under Kara's body.

When Qiana's tongue came into contact with Kara's pussy, she screamed and tightened on Christian's dick, pulling a desperate groan from him. And then he was moving faster, pounding into her, his big hands gripping her shoulders, Qiana's lips sloppily tasting the juncture of their bodies.

"Oh, fuck," Kara moaned, so close to coming again.

This was how it was supposed to be, Kara and Qiana and Christian. Nothing would change, they'd all agreed. Marriage was only a piece of paper; it couldn't define their life or change how they felt about each other. Kara still didn't know if she'd ever believed that or if she said it just because she hoped it could be true. There was no etiquette guide for how to behave when the people you love leave you behind.

Or had she left them?

ON DISPLAY

Pandora Parker

David is doing his enthusiastic best between my legs, with fingers, lips, and tongue. I let out an occasional moan so he feels like I appreciate his attentions but I'm not feeling it tonight. I don't know what's wrong with me lately. I'm lucky. I have a wonderful partner who is more than generous in bed, as well as being an all-around great person. I'm the envy of my friends. They've told me so more than once. I should be happy.

"I want you inside me," I murmur, and he moves up my body and pushes his cock inside me. When he kisses me I can taste my juices on his lips. That used to drive me wild, so why do I feel so detached? I still love him, and as our bodies rock together in urgent rhythm I know we're still good. Perhaps the extra spark just fades with time.

I creep out of bed at 4:30 a.m., taking my clothes to the bathroom to get dressed so I won't disturb David, who is spread out on his back, taking up at least three-quarters of the bed. Fortunately, being only a wish and a promise over five feet, I can still make myself comfortable in the remaining space. But not today. I have work to do.

He's snoring, but it's a snuffly puppy snore rather than the road drill kind. See, even when he's snoring I still think he's cute.

By five I'm on the road. I have a shoot to get to, at a country house out of town. It's about an hour's drive, and we need to catch the early morning light. The forecast is clear, I'm on time, and so far no one has reported any problems.

The sky is lightening as I drive through the impressively large gateway and wend my way up the drive. Mist is emanating from the river on the edge of the grounds. I'm crossing my fingers that we can get set up in time before the rising sun burns it off.

As I pull up to the house I'm reassured by the sight of several cars and a van already parked. Looks like everyone's here.

We're almost done with the garden shoot. I really feel for Janene the model. It's not warm out here, and we're working for a lingerie designer. We have patio heaters but they can't be in shot so she's been running over to huddle next to them whenever she has a break.

When the photographer, Sian, has all the shots she needs we stop for coffee, and that's when things go wrong.

While I'm going through my notes Sian's assistant comes over and tells us that Sherri, our other model, is currently in the bathroom throwing up her breakfast. We still have Janene, but we only have the sizes for the specific model for each set, and although she has a lovely willowy figure, there's no way she'll be able to fill out the corsets meant for Sherri.

"Do you want to cancel?" Sian asks me.

"God no, we can't cancel now. It took me ages to get this

place, not to mention how much it costs. Do you know anyone else who could make it?"

"I don't think so, and even if I did, they wouldn't get here in time."

We sit in silence and stare into our coffees, hoping for inspiration. I feel bad; my first thought was for the job, and not for poor Sherri.

"How is she?"

Sian's assistant Thea answers me.

"She'll be okay. She reckons it was a dodgy takeaway last night."

"Maybe if we just wait for a bit?"

"How much does that underwear cost again?" Sian counters.

"Fair point."

Sian turns to face me.

"Stand up," she says.

"What? Why?"

"Just do it, will you?"

I stand up, and she looks me up and down.

"Maybe you could do it."

"What?" I repeat. "Do what?"

"You're about the same size as Sherri. I reckon you could pull it off."

"No way. There is absolutely no way I'm stripping off for the camera!"

It's about an hour later and I'm standing in a very grand drawing room all trussed in teal silk and cherry-red ribbon. Although the corset means I can't take a deep breath, or sit down, it's oddly comforting. It's impossible to slouch in one of these things. They should be marketed as back supports. My waist looks tiny, but I'm afraid that if I make any sudden movements my breasts will pop right out.

Thea has helped me with the hair and makeup, and I barely recognize the slutty, smoky-eyed temptress I can see in the ornate mirror above the fireplace. Sherri was meant to be modeling the raunchier part of the client's collection. I'm relieved that I don't have to bare my bottom with a thong, but really, the knickers I'm wearing make promises to the imagination that are more rude than if I was wearing nothing at all.

"Ready?" Sian says.

Not in the slightest. But I ignore my fear and say yes.

My first pose involves leaning on the mantelpiece and gazing contemplatively at my reflection with my back curved, bottom thrust out, and legs parted. It feels horribly exposed, but simmering underneath my embarrassment is a sort of fizzy warmth, like champagne bubbles, or butterflies, but it's coming from lower down than my tummy.

I can't believe it.

I think I'm starting to get turned on. I hope to God that none of the crew can tell. Although the thought of people looking at me and realizing how excited I am gives me an even more intense spike of combined pleasure and shame. I don't know what's wrong with me. I've never felt like this before. I'm starting to get wet, and the fine silky material of the knickers I'm wearing is the sort that really shows up damp patches. In this position they'll all be able to see.

It's agony holding the pose, but eventually Sian has enough shots and I can straighten up and close my legs. I'm like a kettle close to the boil for the rest of the shoot, and when we're finished I feel both relieved and incredibly frustrated.

I manage to hold it together until we've packed everything up and the rest of the team has left. I get into the driver's seat of my car and rest my forehead on the steering wheel. I'm going over the shoot in my mind, and instead of starting the car and driving home I take a quick look around. It's a National Trust property, and no one lives on-site. The place is deserted.

I slide the seat back and recline it, stretching out my legs. I take another quick look around. I'm alone, but I'm still worried that someone will appear at any moment.

I'm wearing skinny jeans, which are not at all convenient. I unbutton them and peel them down. I slip my hand into my knickers, closing my eyes and leaning my head back. I remember myself in that first pose, legs parted, like I was on display. I imagine more people there, tourists strolling through, everyone staring while I have to hold my pose.

I'm sliding my fingers through the hot, moist folds around my clit, pushing further down and inside. At the thought of a crowd ogling me there's a gush of wetness and I imagine the silky gusset of the briefs showing a dark patch, signaling my arousal to everyone else in the room.

I push my fingers in and out, faster and faster as I hear people in the crowd.

Oh, my God, look how wet she is!

She's getting off on this, the dirty girl.

Looks like she needs a good seeing to.

Now I'm moaning, riding my hand, fingers inside up to the knuckles, and I'm coming, my muscles in spasm, my cunt clenching on my hand.

I've never had an orgasm quite like that before.

When I get home I feel all sorts of weird. David is visiting his parents and he won't be back until tomorrow evening. Even though I usually miss him like crazy, this time I'm relieved. I need to get my head together before he comes back.

I don't know how he'll feel about me being a stand-in model, and that's before I even think about discussing the effect it had on me. We've never talked about this sort of thing before. Normally I'm so camera shy he can't even get me in a cute couple selfie.

I wonder how strippers deal with this? Do they have a strict work/home life division? Do their partners get jealous? Or turned on?

I tuck myself into bed with a hot chocolate and a book and I read until my eyes won't stay open, but as soon as I turn off the light I'm wide awake again.

I spend most of the night turning and twisting until the duvet has migrated to the bottom of its cover and the sheet has detached itself from the mattress. Around five I finally fall into a deep sleep, not waking until late morning with hazy vision and a stuffed-up nose.

After giving myself first aid in the form of espresso I check my email.

Sian has already sent me a link to the raw photos from yesterday. I have to go through them and pick out the ones for her to edit and send on to the client.

The exterior shots are easy. I've run enough of these things to know just what the client wants, so it doesn't take me long to tag the best ones.

I feel queasy as I hover the pointer over the interior shoot folder. What if they're awful? But surely Sian would have said something by now. It's silly but my heart is racing and my hands are shaking.

I double-click on the folder and the thumbnails ripple across my screen. I expand the first one and I'm immediately confronted with a view of my bottom. She must have taken it from a low angle. It's rather . . . curvaceous. Certainly the lingerie seems to be well displayed. I was worried about not being tanned enough, but the pale skin of my bare thighs contrasts beautifully with the teal silk briefs and the dark lace-top stockings. My legs are braced straight and my ankles and calves look slim and shapely atop the stiletto heels.

Looking at the pictures brings back that fizzy feeling of arousal from yesterday. I close the laptop and try to distract myself. I don't know which ones to choose. It's impossible to be objective when looking at photos of myself, not to mention the fact that my libido seems to be trying to take over my brain at the moment.

The photos can wait. I need to think about what I'm going to tell David.

It's after dark when David gets home. He walks in and sheds shoes, coat, and bag at apparently random points. He stretches, grazing the ceiling with his fingertips and displaying a couple of inches of pleasingly muscular stomach. Like always when he's been away, he declares that he's starving before enfolding me in a hug and nibbling my neck and ears. I would usually laugh but tonight I'm too tense.

He pulls back and looks at me, frowning.

"What's up?"

"Can we talk?"

"Um, okay. Should I be worried?" He sits down on the sofa. I sit opposite, hugging my knees to my chest.

"We had a bit of an emergency on location today." I give him an edited version of what happened. As he's listening, his expression veers between apprehensive, confused, and relieved.

"I thought you were about to give me the push," he confesses, and the idea of him leaving reminds me just how much I love him.

"I was worried you'd be upset, you know, about me being

photographed in my knickers. Well, not mine, they belong to the client. That sounds even worse! You know what I mean."

"I think it's amazing. Everyone should see how gorgeous and sexy you are." He enfolds me in a hug, nuzzling my neck with kisses and little bites. "Do I get to see these photos then?"

"Actually, I was wondering if you could help me pick the ones to send to the client. I can usually assess which ones are best but it's really hard looking at pictures of myself!"

I retrieve my laptop and we settle down on the sofa to look through them together. The one already onscreen is my first pose, with my bottom thrust out provocatively. Sian has framed it so it seems as if I'm looking at the viewer through the mirror, sleepy-eyed and knowing.

David is quiet.

"So, what do you think?"

He whistles softly. I glance down and see the shape of his erection under his jeans, and the idea of him being turned on by my pictures ignites a wave of heat starting between my legs and rising to flush my chest and face. I don't know whether I feel embarrassed or incredibly turned on or both at once.

"I'm thinking I might not last long enough to look through them. Why don't we go to bed and go through them later?"

"I've got a better idea. You keep looking at those photos. I need to know which ones are best. I'll help you concentrate."

I undo his jeans, pulling down the front of his boxers so his cock can spring out of the confinement of his clothes. I cradle his balls with one hand and lower my head, taking the end into my mouth and swirling my tongue around the tip. He moans as I take him a little deeper, my lips tight around his shaft.

I push my other hand between my legs for the second time today. I'm already dripping wet. I make my fingers into a "V" shape, squeezing my clit between them.

He pushes his hands into my hair, tugging gently, just the way he knows I like it. I take him as deep as I can until I feel the smooth tip nudging the back of my throat. His hips start to thrust and he gasps a warning that he's about to come, but I hold him in my mouth. I love that moment when he can no longer stop himself, and I'm rewarded seconds later as my mouth is filled, the warm, salty liquid spilling out over my chin. It's enough to send me over the edge into a shuddering climax, thighs squeezing my hand tight, my face pushed into his lap.

Neither of us speak for what seems like ages. I'm floating in a post-orgasmic languor when David finally says, "Did I ever tell you I was really into photography when I was in high school?"

"I don't think so." I'm on the verge of sleep, but his next words cause me to open my eyes and look at him properly.

"Maybe I should take it up again." He's got a mischievous smile on his face.

"Maybe you'll need a model."

"And maybe that model would like to dress up in different costumes?"

"I think the model would enjoy that."

"Actually, I've always wanted to see you all buttoned up in Victorian dress but I was afraid to ask."

"Really? Well, so long as you'll be unbuttoning me afterward and besmirching my honor, I think that can be arranged."

He leans down and kisses me long and slow and I realize I'm not sleepy after all.

My friends think I'm lucky. They don't know the half of it.

ABOUT THE
AUTHORS

ANGELA ADDAMS (angelaaddams.com) is an author of many naughty things. She believes that the written word is an amazing tool for crafting the most erotic of scenarios and tells stories about people getting down and dirty and falling in love. She loves anything covered in chocolate . . . except for bugs.

MELANIE ANTON is a former adult performer living in Southern California with her spouse and as many cats as possible. She writes steamy stories and humorous speculative fiction.

CHRISTINA BERRY (christinaberry.com) writes sex-positive, contemporary romance. Her debut novel, *Up for Air*, won "Sexiest Consent" in the 2021 Good Sex Awards and other honors. A citizen of the Cherokee Nation, Christina is originally from Oklahoma, and currently resides in Austin, Texas, with her husband and two robot cats.

PANDORA PARKER is an English writer of erotic short stories and poetry, who lives in a small seaside town in South Wales. She thinks that erotic fiction can and should be just as well written as literary or genre fiction, and that is her aim.

LIN DEVON is a mixed-race pansexual bibliophilic sci-fi, fantasy, and horror fan more at home in a book sipping hot tea with cats than just about anywhere. Her previous work can be found in *Best Women's Erotica of the Year Volume 8, The Big Book of Orgasms, Volume 2,* and *Crowded House.*

D. FOSTALOVE has been published in numerous anthologies, including *Cunning Linguists, Erato: Flash Fiction,* and *The Big Book of Orgasms, Volume 2.* He was awarded in the inaugural Good Sex Awards in the "Best Sexy Talk" category. He's the author of *When I Miss You* and *50-50.*

JODIE GRIFFIN (jodiegriffin.com) is a contemporary romance author who writes naughty tales about nice girls and the people who love them. She is also an avid photographer and easy-trail hiker whose life is fueled by anxiety and chocolate.

VIX HILLE is the pseudonym of an extensively published author who is trying to get back into writing after a few years away.

KATRINA JACKSON is a college professor by day who writes erotica, erotic romance, and historical fiction in her spare time. She writes racially diverse and often queer stories that show love and the world in all its beauty and colors.

R. MAGDALEN (IG: @r.magdalen.erotica) writes short stories and poems about queer joy and sex. They live on the top of a windy hill in a medium-sized city.

LOU MORGAN is a Black Scottish woman with a passion for lesbian stories, middle-aged actresses, and Doc Martens. She publishes feminist non-fiction and children's writing under a different name.

QUENBY (quenbycreatives.com) is an award-winning queer writer and activist based in the UK. They use erotica as a way to explore the way fatness, disability, and kink shape queer intimacy and sexuality.

BIRCH ROSEN (birchrosen.com) lives in the Seattle area. Their poetry and prose have appeared in *Michigan Quarterly Review*, *just femme & dandy*, and *Bellevue Literary Review*. Rosen is the author of *Boobless, T&A (Transitioning & Attractiveness)*, and the Trans Restroom Rants series.

LEAH SAGE is a Texas-born cowgirl that has been many places, known many people, seen many things, and learned so much more. Wife, writer, gamer, part-time philosopher, painter, and Reiki Master, Leah writes many genres and many subjects, but her guilty pleasure has always been erotica.

RAE SHAWN (loveraeshawn.com) writes captivating, inclusive contemporary Black romances that'll have you up-in-arms for the heroes and, sometimes, even the villains. When she isn't writing, she's dancing her way around her living room or watching reruns of *Supernatural* and early-aughts anime. Find her on Twitter, TikTok, and Instagram at @raeshawnstories.

SJ SWEET BREAD (they/he) is a demi boy, who is learning to breathe underwater and bake without a recipe. He sometimes writes, but mostly he is wasting time watching *Bob's Burgers* or *Twin Peaks* (basically the same show).

A criminal defense attorney by day, **NOEL STEVENS** writes romances featuring positive portrayals of criminal justice reform and HEAs for public defenders, activists, and criminal justice-involved individuals. She lives in the southwest United States with her husband and their two dogs.

KELVIN SPARKS (KelvinSparks.com) is a writer, sex toy reviewer, trans man, and pervert based in London, UK. He loves writing sci-fi and fantasy erotica (especially if it gives him an excuse for self-indulgent worldbuilding), as well as stories about transmasculine characters.

AUSTIN WORLEY (austinworleywriter.wordpress.com) is an author of fantasy, science fiction, and romance just beginning to explore erotica. When not writing, he enjoys reading, gaming, and amateur astronomy.

ABOUT
THE EDITOR

RACHEL KRAMER BUSSEL (rachelkramerbussel.com) is a New Jersey-based author, editor, blogger, and writing instructor. She has edited over seventy books of erotica, including *Crowded House Threesome and Group Sex Erotica; It Takes Two; Coming Soon: Women's Orgasm Erotica; Dirty Dates: Erotic Fantasies for Couples; Come Again: Sex Toy Erotica; The Big Book of Orgasms*, Volumes 1 and 2; *The Big Book of Submission*, Volumes 1 and 2; *Lust in Latex; Anything for You; Baby Got Back: Anal Erotica; Suite Encounters; Gotta Have It; Women in Lust; Surrender; Orgasmic; Fast Girls; Going Down; Tasting Him; Tasting Her; Crossdressing; Cheeky Spanking Stories; Bottoms Up; Spanked: Red-Cheeked Erotica; Please, Sir; Please, Ma'am; He's on Top; She's on Top; Best Bondage Erotica of the Year*, Volumes 1 and 2; and *Best Women's Erotica of the Year*, Volumes 1-8. Her anthologies have won eight IPPY (Independent Publisher) Awards, and *The Big Book of Submission, Volume 2, Dirty Dates,* and

Surrender won the National Leather Association Samois Anthology Award. She is the recipient of the 2021 National Leather Association John Preston Short Fiction Award.

Rachel has written for *AVN, Bust, Cosmopolitan, Curve,* The Daily Beast, Elle.com, Forbes.com, Fortune.com, *Glamour,* The Goods, Gothamist, *Harper's Bazaar,* Huffington Post, *Inked, InStyle, Marie Claire, MEL, Men's Health, Newsday, New York Post, New York Observer, The New York Times, O: The Oprah Magazine, Penthouse, The Philadelphia Inquirer,* Refinery29, *Rolling Stone,* The Root, Salon, *San Francisco Chronicle, Self,* Slate, Time.com, *Time Out New York,* and *Zink,* among others. She has appeared on "The Gayle King Show," "The Martha Stewart Show," "The Berman and Berman Show," NY1, and Showtime's "Family Business." She hosted the popular In the Flesh Erotic Reading Series, featuring readers from Susie Bright to Zane, speaks at conferences, and does readings and teaches erotic writing workshops around the world and online. She blogs at lustylady.blogspot.com and consults about erotica and sex-related nonfiction at eroticawriting101.com. Follow her @raquelita on Twitter.